Guilt swamped Madison.

She'd been sitting there, having different thoughts, silly thoughts, about a guy she hardly knew and who had helped her out once. He'd given her no real sign or indication that he gave her a passing thought. But even though she'd tried to fight it, and ignore it, she knew that he was stirring something in her that she hadn't felt in a long time.

Part of her was horrified. This wasn't Fletch's issue. This was hers. Maybe she was just reaching that stage—the one where she might consider moving on, trying to meet someone else. But even as the thought fully formed in her brain, she still felt weighed down with guilt. What if people thought three years wasn't long enough?

She didn't even know if it was. She just knew for the first time in forever, she was attracted to someone again. There. She'd admitted it.

Dear Reader,

There's something so exciting about setting a book in a foreign climate—and even more exciting when you haven't actually been there and need to research! I'm flying to Australia later this year and when I saw how fabulous Changi Airport was, I was definitely tempted to do a stopover!

This book features Madison Koh, a Scottish girl who settled in Singapore and whose husband died just after the birth of her twins. Maddie is a physiotherapist and wants all her colleagues to know that, a few years on, she can still do her job and cope on her own with twins.

Arthur Fletcher—known as Fletch—arrives from the US to work as a pediatrician. Fletch is a good guy, with a number of exes, but he's just never met The One. Until he meets Madison Koh. Neither of them is looking for a serious romance, and both of them know they're not a good match for each other. But as sparks fly and temperatures rise, neither can deny how they really feel.

I love happy-ever-afters and hope that you'll like this one. If you want to get in touch, you can contact me via my website, www.scarlet-wilson.com.

Love,

Scarlet

A DADDY
FOR HER TWINS

SCARLET WILSON

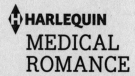

HARLEQUIN

MEDICAL
ROMANCE

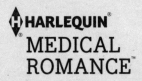

HARLEQUIN®
MEDICAL
ROMANCE™

Recycling programs
for this product may
not exist in your area.

ISBN-13: 978-1-335-59492-1

A Daddy for Her Twins

Copyright © 2023 by Scarlet Wilson

Harlequin Enterprises ULC
22 Adelaide St. West, 41st Floor
Toronto, Ontario M5H 4E3, Canada
www.Harlequin.com

Printed in U.S.A.

Scarlet Wilson wrote her first story aged eight and has never stopped. She's worked in the health service for more than thirty years, having trained as a nurse and a health visitor. Scarlet now works in public health and lives on the west coast of Scotland with her fiancé and their two sons. Writing medical romances and contemporary romances is a dream come true for her.

Books by Scarlet Wilson

Harlequin Medical Romance

California Nurses
Nurse with a Billion Dollar Secret

Night Shift in Barcelona
The Night They Never Forgot

Neonatal Nurses
Neonatal Doc on Her Doorstep

Marriage Miracle in Emergency
Snowed In with the Surgeon

Visit the Author Profile page
at Harlequin.com for more titles.

This book is dedicated to the fabulous vaccination team staff I work with, some of whom gave me tips about Singapore! Thank you, Elaine x.

Praise for
Scarlet Wilson

"Charming and oh so passionate, *Cinderella and the Surgeon* was everything I love about Harlequin Medicals. Author Scarlet Wilson created a flowing story rich with flawed but likable characters and… will be sure to delight readers and have them sighing happily with that sweet ending."
—*Harlequin Junkie*

Scarlet Wilson won the 2017 RoNA Rose Award for her book
***Christmas in the Boss's Castle*.**

CHAPTER ONE

ARTHUR FLETCHER WAS TIRED. More than tired. And it was all entirely his own fault. He'd landed at Singapore Changi airport, remembered he'd been told it was the finest in the world, and lost himself in the dazzling array of butterfly gardens, canopy park, waterfall fountains, not to mention the delicious eateries and shopping opportunities.

He'd been warned of course. But Arthur had decided—instead of immediately grabbing his suitcase and leaving the airport as he'd done on every other occasion in cities all around the world—he would take some time to enjoy the experience.

If everything worked out the way it should, it would likely be two years before he was back at Changi airport and moving on to a new post. St David's Children's Hospital—where he'd landed his latest paediatrician post—was only five years old and was already developing an illustrious reputation around the world. Set in one of Singapore's busiest districts, it rarely had empty beds, and the teaching and learning opportunities were vast. The chance of the promotion had appealed, as had the chance to go back to Singapore—a place he'd loved and worked in before.

Everything would have been great if he'd actually managed to collect the keys to his apartment and move in as planned. But it seemed that life had decided to throw him a few spanners and he'd unexpectedly ended up in a hotel overnight. He was just hoping he could get things sorted out quickly.

He tugged at the collar of his short-sleeved shirt, trying to adjust to the warmer climate again. His appointment as a paediatric consultant who would be involved with the doctors' training programme at St David's had gone smoothly. He'd worked previously in Singapore after qualifying as a doctor, and after taking an appointment in the US, and then in Germany, he'd been pleasantly surprised to be headhunted for the new role.

His official meeting and tour of the hospital wasn't until ten o'clock, but his late-night ventures at Changi airport had made him edgy about oversleeping, meaning he hadn't really slept at all. He'd finally got dressed just after seven, and was now sitting in the main entranceway of the hospital, in the visitors' café.

Even though it was early, the streets of Singapore had been bustling, and the hospital foyer was entirely the same. He knew there was a shift change, with staff leaving and entering in a whole rainbow variety of scrubs. Scrub colour was usually dependent on role, and there were a few he hadn't yet identified.

His phone buzzed and he had a quick check. He gave a sigh and sent a text back. Lisa. He also noticed a message from Jess. He sent her a message back too. Both ex-girlfriends. Fletch had a habit of being a serial dater who could never last longer than six months. He was always up front about it. He had no plans to settle down in the near future, and when any relationship he was in reached that 'next stage' point, he always had the hard conversation and walked away amicably.

He'd lived all his adult life like this. While he'd like eventually to have a family of his own, he just didn't feel ready yet—likely because of his own upbringing as a child. His mother had dated a few men after his father had left, always saying she was 'trying before buying'. It had taken her a while to finally meet his stepfather and settle down. And the behaviour had kind of imprinted on Fletch.

Most of his exes had moved on successfully with no hard feelings. He was lucky like that. But they all kept telling him one day he would meet 'the one'. Fletch gave a smile and put his phone back in his pocket. Maybe in a few years.

As he sipped his coffee, he could feel the buzz through his body. He was excited about this new job. Excited about moving back to Singapore for a spell. He'd always loved this country, with its pleasant climate, friendly people and world of opportunities.

He watched as there was some jostling near the main entrance. A woman had her hands full, holding the hand of one young child, the other, grasped in her arms was clearly having a bad day, and she was struggling with a stroller and several bags.

He stood up without thinking and automatically walked over. 'You've got your hands full, let me help you.'

She blinked as she blew a wayward strand of hair out of her eyes. Fletch was always cautious when offering to assist, knowing that some people didn't appreciate it, but this lady was different.

'Brilliant,' she said, placing her squirming child in his arms. 'Meet Mr Cranky, also known as Justin.' She rejigged her bags, organising them on her stroller, and nodded to the young girl beside her. 'This is Mia.' She wrinkled her nose as she kept walking, now keeping the stroller under control. 'I'm Madison, I don't think we've met before.'

She was wearing a pair of navy scrubs, her light brown hair tied up in a ponytail and he could see freckles on her nose. She also had a hint of an accent. Scottish? Irish? He wasn't sure.

'Arthur Fletcher,' he said, walking alongside. Mr Cranky was looking at him suspiciously, but hadn't yet objected to being held by a stranger. 'I'm starting as a paediatrician this morning.'

Her footsteps slowed for a second and she gave him a broad smile. 'You are? That's fantastic. You'll love it here,' she said without hesitation, and then looked a bit thoughtful. 'I'll see you, then.' She glanced down at her scrubs. 'I'm one of the physios and part of my role is rehab, so I'm sometimes on the children's unit.' She looked over at Justin and gave a sigh.

'I don't know what's going on with my boy these last few days. He's been cranky and irritable.' She held up a hand and laughed before Fletch could speak. 'No, I'm not asking you to look at him. He's just out of sorts. Nothing serious.'

Fletch smiled. 'So, I'm Arthur Fletcher. But call me Fletch. The only person who calls me Arthur is my grandad.'

Madison's eyes twinkled. 'Named after him?' There was something about those eyes...

He nodded. 'You got it.'

They reached the elevators and she pressed a button. 'We're heading to the crèche. Have you been shown around yet?'

He shook his head. 'Well, allow me.' She smiled. 'You might as well know where the crèche is, as they'll hold some of your potential clientele.'

He nodded as the elevator rose, trying not to notice the shadows under Madison's eyes, or the paleness of her skin. She was clearly tired. But he didn't want to ask intrusive questions.

'I love your accent,' he said.

She laughed. 'Scots. But I'm not really sure why. My mum and dad are both from

Scotland, but Dad was part of the British Consulate so I've lived all over the world.'

'You have?' He adjusted Justin, letting the little guy fold into his neck.

'Germany, Italy.' She nodded her head. 'We were in Singapore twice. I did most of my high school time here and always knew I wanted to come back.'

'So, you live here for good now?'

She nodded towards her children. 'Family ties. I love it here.'

He looked again. Her children clearly had some Asian heritage and his eyes went immediately to her hand. No ring. But he assumed nothing. He knew better than to do that.

The elevator doors pinged open and she led him down the corridor to a brightly coloured room, where children were clearly separated by age. The crèche was well staffed and children were signed in and out. A staff member came over with her arms outstretched to take Justin. 'How's my favourite?' she said to him as Madison's daughter skipped off to play with some friends. 'Did they have a good time in Scotland with your parents?' she asked Madison.

'They loved it,' she replied quickly. 'But getting them back into a routine is proving a challenge. This is Jen,' said Madison, 'and this is Fletch, one of the new children's doctors who was gracious enough to help me.'

Jen's eyes flicked over to Fletch with a hint of curiosity. 'Nice to meet you,' she said as she stroked Justin's hair. She glanced back to Madison. 'Still feeling a bit off?'

Madison nodded and took a deep breath. 'He didn't sleep well last night—well, none of us did. But he was just unsettled. I honestly wonder if he's a bit jet-lagged. They've only been back three days. No temperature, no cough. Just...irritable.'

Jen gave a brief nod. 'Don't worry, I'll keep him close, and call you if I'm worried at all. You okay if I let him sleep today?'

'Of course,' said Madison. She watched as Jen walked away with Justin, talking gently in his ear. Fletch could see the strain on her face.

Like any mother she was clearly worried. He knew it was none of his business, but did she have any help? And why was he even wondering? He hadn't even met this woman for more than five minutes and he had the weirdest feeling around her—almost as if she were pulling him in, and making him curious.

His phone buzzed as they walked back

down the corridor. 'Where are you headed?' she asked as the elevator doors opened again.

He glanced at his phone. 'Finally, keys for my apartment.'

She raised her eyebrows. 'You haven't moved in already?'

'No, there was a bit of a hiccup and I stayed in a hotel last night.'

She folded her arms, looking amused. He was almost relieved to see the worry lines disappear from her face. 'That sounds like a story.'

'It is.' He turned his phone around and showed her the apartment.

'Wow.' She took the phone from his hand and started swiping through the photos, then gave a shudder and laughed. She handed the phone back. 'Too much glass for a mother of two three-year-olds.'

Fletch gave a conciliatory nod. 'You're right. I'll spend two years trying not to touch it at all. But I'm happy with the amenities. There's a gym, a swimming pool and a garden.' He rolled his eyes. 'All I really needed was the keys.'

'So, what happened, then?'

'The agent got delayed. His flight got cancelled and his partner's father was sick.' He held up his hands. 'I wasn't going to go to another hospital to harass someone for keys when their father was sick, so I said I'd book into a hotel for a night or so.'

'So, you get your keys today?'

'Thankfully, yes. I'll need to do some shopping. Get a few bits and pieces, and some food.' He paused for a second, and then just asked. 'Would you be able to point me in the right direction? I've been to Singapore before, but stayed in a different part, so I'm not as familiar with the shops and markets near where I'm staying.'

She waved her hand as the elevator doors opened, depositing them at the paediatric unit. 'Absolutely no problem. Give me a shout before you finish today and I'll give you a list of where, and when, to shop.'

He opened his mouth to ask what she meant, but she winked at him and disappeared into another room.

Fletch gave an amused laugh and walked down the corridor, shaking his head, not quite sure what to make of Madison.

She was friendly, obviously had her hands full, but there was something else about her. He was intrigued. He wanted to ask questions. But could well be reading things that weren't there at all. Maybe he was still jet-lagged? Yes, that was it. Once he'd given himself a few days to meet people, and see around the city again, he might finally get his head on straight.

A woman appeared in front of him, with a steely demeanour. She looked him up and down, and he realised instantly he hadn't collected his ID badge yet. 'Dr Fletcher,' he said, holding out his hand. 'I'm the new paediatrician, and Madison—' he gave a sideways glance to see if she was anywhere in sight, '—had started to show me round.'

The woman's nose wrinkled for a second as she clearly decided if she was on board or not. 'Rui Lee,' she said quickly, 'Sister of the Paediatric Unit. Come with me, Dr Fletcher. I think you have a meeting in a few hours.'

He held in a grimace and followed the fleet-footed woman down the corridor. As he looked out over the city landscape he couldn't help but smile. From the moment he'd set foot in St David's this morning he'd had a good feeling. A vibe. Something that was hard to explain. But he could see it in the faces around him. Staff wanted to be here. People wanted to work here. There was no drama. No chaos or rush. Everything seemed controlled. Parents were at the sides of the beds with children. Staff were intermingled amongst them. He could hear short bursts of childhood laughter, and low voices murmuring around him.

Inquisitive medical students, clearly wearing new white coats, were gathered around a whiteboard in a room as a pharmacist was going through the chemistry aspect of medications. In another room, he saw some student nurses in mid-discussion with a tutor about childhood vaccinations. Teaching sessions weren't confined to universities or lecture halls. Teaching was happening directly on the wards. This was the reason he'd come here. This was part of the programme he was to lead, and he could already see the benefits before his eyes.

The good feeling kept rolling through his body as Sister Lee took him along the corridor towards the management offices. 'Settled in?' she asked over her shoulder.

He was slightly surprised at the social question. She'd seemed the tiniest bit hostile. 'Eh, almost,' he said. 'I had a bit of an issue getting access to the apartment I've rented. But hopefully that's solved now. I spent last night in a hotel, but I couldn't really sleep, so I arrived here early and had a coffee.'

She gave him a curious glance. 'So, you don't already know Madison Koh?'

Ah, so this was why she was being sociable. He shook his head. 'I met her downstairs for the first time.' He gave a soft laugh. 'She seemed to have her hands full so I offered to help.'

This time the glance he was shot was careful. 'Madison is one of our best physios. She does have her hands full. It's such a shame that she lost her husband a few years ago.'

His footsteps faltered but he quickly recovered. His brain automatically going into backwards mode, making sure he hadn't blundered unintentionally when talking to Madison. He didn't think so.

'That's such a shame. She seems a very nice woman. I'm looking forward to working with her.'

Rui's eyes were steady. 'She is a very nice woman. Her husband was a radiologist here. He's missed. We're all lucky in a way, because we get to see their children every day. I can see elements of Jason in each of his children.'

'That's nice.' Fletch meant that sincerely. 'I'm glad you mentioned it,' he added. 'I would have hated to put my foot in it around Madison.' His steps slowed as they reached the management offices.

'I'll leave you here,' said Rui. 'It was nice to meet you. I'll go over some procedures and electronic systems with you later.' She gave him a half-smile. 'Hope you get your apartment situation sorted out.'

She left him next to an unusual arched window that gave a spectacular view of the city landscape. He stood for a few moments, his head full of what he'd just heard. Madison seemed nice. Now he understood why she looked so tired. She was on her own.

He knew it shouldn't matter. But she was a colleague, so it did. He made a note to be mindful where he could when working together. For the second time today it struck him how curious he was about her, and he shook his head as he tried to imagine why he was drawn to this new colleague. A pull. That was all he could describe it as.

Smiling to himself, with one more glance at Singapore, his new home, he knocked on the door.

Madison finished typing up her notes and checked her emails for new referrals. Her hair had escaped from its too-loose hair scrunchie again and she attempted to tame it back into some kind of submission. A text appeared on the watch on her wrist and she had a quick glance. It was the crèche, reassuring her that Justin had settled. Thank goodness.

It was odd. She couldn't quite put her finger on what was wrong with her son, she just knew he wasn't himself. There wasn't anything to scare her, or to make her rush to her own paediatrician. There was just... something.

He was irritable. He was restless, and, even though he was clearly tired at times, he didn't sleep well—which then meant that no one slept well. She'd checked all the usual things. His temperature was fine. He was eating and drinking. Peeing and pooing. He had no unusual rashes. He was up to date with his vaccinations. And there were no outbreaks of any normal childhood diseases that she knew about. She'd even sounded his chest. But still, there was nothing to explain why her boy wasn't his usual self.

Madison had worked hard at keeping a happy work-life balance since the death of her husband. She was careful to give equal attention to her children, and happily had the ongoing help from her in-laws. She used the crèche while at work, and the twins were enrolled for nursery and due to start soon.

But the sleepless nights were getting to her. She'd thankfully accepted the offer from her in-laws to have Justin and Mia overnight. The whole family had shared her devastation when Jason had been killed in a cycling accident, a few months after their children had arrived. Her parents had arrived from Scotland, and Jason's sister and parents had flocked around her, helping her keep things together and continue to function.

Her parents had finally needed to return to Scotland, but continued to visit and had even taken their grandchildren back to Scotland for a few holidays to help Madison out with childcare when necessary. The kids were just back from a fortnight with her mum and dad in the Scottish Highlands. Her in-laws were also there on a weekly basis, always only a telephone call away. She was lucky. She knew that. But learning to adjust to life without Jason had taken some time.

Now, she was getting there. The perpetual sadness had started to lift. She was determined to not miss out on the joy of her children and making memories with them. It helped she'd continued to work in the same place. There were no awkward questions from her colleagues. They knew her circumstances. They accepted her and her children with open arms and she was eternally grateful.

She lifted one of the nearby slimline tablets, logged in, and pulled up the referrals. Two from Paediatrics and two from the adult rehab ward. She already had ten patients on her list, but she could cope with four new referrals. She might even have time to grab a snack today. She took off her watch and tucked it into her pocket alongside the tablet, heading down to the wards.

By the time she'd finished her adult patients, the lack of sleep from last night was starting to hit her in all the worst ways. She hurried into Paeds and gave Rui a wave before ducking into the staffroom to heat up some soup. The staffroom was filled with comfortable sofas, a sink, microwave, and coffee machine. Madison set the timer for two minutes and sat down on a bright red sofa, considering the box of snacks in the middle of the table. The staffroom was empty. Most staff had already had their lunch by now and she was running late.

A hand touched her shoulder and she bolted to her feet, eyes wide, head going from side to side.

'Sorry.' Fletch was standing behind her, looking sheepish. He'd changed into a set of green scrubs and had his hospital ID clipped to his uniform now and his name badge on his chest.

For a few seconds her brain tried to compute. She recognised him, of course. But he looked different in his doctor scrubs than he had in his shirt and suit trousers. Scrubs seemed to reveal more. Whether anyone wanted them to or not.

Fletch had a broad frame, defined shoulders and muscular arms. He worked out. There was no flab. This guy worked out. With the v in his scrubs she could see a peek of chest hair and alongside a hint of a tan. Did he work out with nothing on? And why were the only words that would register in her brain 'work out'?

Madison gave herself a jolt, as her brain tried to settle. She couldn't remember the last time she'd let her thoughts linger on the physical attributes of a male colleague. What was wrong with her?

He remained apologetic. 'I didn't mean to wake you.'

Heat flooded her body and she could feel it in her cheeks. She was embarrassed. Of course, she was. She'd never fallen asleep at work before. That was disgraceful. She was on duty. She was supposed to be seeing patients. And this guy was brand new—what on earth would he think of her?

'I wasn't sleeping,' she said automatically without thinking. Denial seeming like the best defence.

He winced. 'You were snoring.'

The heat in her cheeks multiplied and she could feel tears brimming in her eyes. She'd worked so hard to keep her reputation impeccable at work, especially because her colleagues knew everything she'd gone through. The last thing she wanted anyone to think was that she couldn't cope being a single parent, or that she wasn't doing the best job possible for her and Jason's kids. Even the thought of that made her heart ache.

Somehow, falling asleep at work seemed to fit in the category of not coping.

'I don't snore!' she snapped.

Fletch jerked backwards as if he'd been stung. She could almost see a shield forming in front of him as he straightened. 'Of course, no problem. I'll leave you to it.' He turned and walked out of the room without another word and Madison cringed.

Her stomach growled as she stepped over to the microwave, her appetite gone. She stared at the soup for two minutes and then poured it down the sink, putting the carton in the bin.

She closed her hands over her face for a few minutes and took a few deep breaths.

Get it together, she told herself.

She tried to be rational. Okay, so she'd now just snapped at—and likely offended—the new doctor, who, from this morning's meeting, had seemed like a perfectly nice bloke. He was going to think—she couldn't even imagine what he might think, but this was someone she wanted to have a professional, respectful relationship with. She didn't want awkwardness, or tension. She certainly didn't want him to write her off as either someone to feel sorry for, or someone who might be unreliable because he'd caught her sleeping at work.

She sat back down and leaned her head forward into her hands. She was tired. She was overtired and, hopefully, that would be sorted for her tonight, thanks to her in-laws.

Her stomach growled and she absent-mindedly opened the biscuit box and took one. The very last thing she needed to happen was to go back to work and start to be light-headed because she hadn't eaten.

The biscuit was gone in two bites and she

stood up, brushed her uniform down and washed her hands.

She took herself back out onto the ward. Rui Lee was discussing a patient with another member of staff, and Madison gathered some equipment to assess her two new patients. By the time she'd gathered what she needed, Rui was finished.

'I'm going to do the two new assessments.' She took a breath and tilted her chin. 'Is Dr Fletcher still around? I wondered if he might want to observe as part of his orientation?'

Rui gave her a careful look. 'He's gone down to Radiology. He wants another set of films on a child and wanted to see if they could be shot another way.'

Her eyes were steady on Madison. It made her feel as if Rui were steadily unpeeling her skin like an onion. She'd taken other new employees with her as part of their orientation, so it wasn't that unusual for her to show someone around. 'No problem,' she said with a forced cheeriness she didn't normally have to use at work. Again—what was wrong with her?

She was aware she'd been feeling restless lately—wondering if it was time to start thinking of herself as a woman again, and not just a mother. Her thoughts always went back to one thing—was she ready? It was hard to know, but her mind was starting to go places it hadn't in the last few years, maybe her brain was trying to tell her something?

She disappeared to assess her patients, concentrating only on work for the next few hours. The words about Fletch going down to Radiology made her the tiniest bit uncomfortable and it was utterly ridiculous. Radiology was where her husband, Jason, had worked. She could imagine them both meeting. Discussing the possibility of different films to get a better view of the issue. Jason would have bent over backwards to ensure his service assisted in the best possible way for a patient's outcome.

She swallowed, a lump in her throat. She'd tried hard over the last two years to keep those kinds of thoughts in a careful place. The first time she'd walked back into work after Jason's death had been like a throat punch. She'd almost turned around and walked back out. But she couldn't do that. She had a family to support. Children to bring up. A life to lead.

Her workmates had all been a great help. And, in Madison's head, she still just took things a day at a time.

She had moved on. She didn't spend all

day thinking about Jason. Sometimes, when one of the kids did something, she saw a glint of Jason in them. It was amazing the mannerisms that seemed to be inbuilt—the twins had been too small to have any real memories of their father—but occasionally one, or both, of them would do something that really reminded her of Jason. It gave her comfort. It reassured her that she still had a little part of him.

The first few times it broke her heart. But now, the pain wasn't raw. He would always hold a piece of her heart. But she couldn't spend the rest of her life grieving. She was happy to be settled with the children and getting on with her life. If only she could get to the bottom of what was going on with Justin.

CHAPTER TWO

MADISON HAD BEEN partly relieved she hadn't seen Fletch for a few days. But it was clear he was certainly making waves—of the good kind.

Everywhere she went, someone mentioned the handsome, friendly paediatrician who was making friends throughout the hospital.

'He doesn't really know anyone here yet,' she heard one of the nurses on the rehab unit say.

'Didn't he work in Singapore before?' asked another.

Madison hid her smile. It was clear that word was getting around about the new doc. It was always interesting watching the hospital grapevine from the sidelines rather than actually being part of it.

'I'm sure he did,' said the original nurse. 'But it was another hospital in another part of the city. I think he knows some of the consultants though.'

Madison held up her tablet. 'I have a patient to see, and he's one of Fletch's. Does anyone know where he is? This is a new referral and I'd like to get a bit of background before I start.'

'He's just gone to the cafeteria,' said a passing support worker. 'I passed him on the stairs.'

Madison glanced at her watch. She could do with a coffee, having missed breakfast this morning, and although she would usually just grab one in the staffroom, she was more anxious to have a chat about this patient.

'I'll go and find him,' she said with a wave of her hand and made her way out of the ward and down the stairs. As she entered the cafeteria, Fletch was exchanging pleasantries with another of the consultants and she wondered if she could interrupt, or if this was work talk. But Fletch caught her gaze and waved her over. He didn't exactly look delighted to see her—maybe her slightly snarky behaviour before had created a bad impression. Darn it. Not exactly ideal when she had to work with this guy—as well as muddle through her feelings.

She gave both doctors a beaming smile as she grabbed a croissant and a coffee, determined to give him a new perspective of her. 'Hi, Fletch, I wanted to catch you about the new patient you referred. Is now a good time, or will I see you back on the ward?'

'No problem,' Fletch said immediately as the other doc's page sounded and he headed off. 'Let's grab a table.'

She sat down opposite him and put some jam on her croissant, hoping for a quick burst of energy from the calories. He had a big pile of muesli and some bacon on a side plate.

His phone buzzed as he sat it on the table and he looked, but ignored it. He took a few spoonfuls of muesli. 'So, what kind of regime would you normally put Adrian on?'

Madison took a sip of her coffee. Straight to the patient, part of her liked that, and part of her wondered if he didn't want to do niceties with her because of her previous snarkiness. She took a breath and started succinctly. 'It's difficult. I checked his records but can't find a history of where he's been treated before. Cystic fibrosis is a difficult disease and it's always tougher when a child moves into your area and you can't get a realistic picture of the history of the disease for your patient.'

He nodded in agreement. 'His parents were staying in Italy, so I think it will be some time before we get to see his records, and we'll need them translated too. I took a verbal history from them—' he spun around a notebook he'd taken from his pocket '—and will be the first to admit that I don't know the standards for treatment for CF in that country. I'm going to have to hope it's based on the same worldwide information that we know.'

Madison gave a nod as his phone beeped again. 'I'll check his films before I start chest physio this morning. And I'll go easy to begin with.'

'I'll maybe come along. His chest is very congested.' He picked up his phone and sighed.

'You're popular.' She smiled.

He gave a rueful smile. 'This is what happens when you're an eternal bachelor and stay friends with all your exes.'

Madison was a little taken aback and started laughing. 'You stay friends with them all?' This information should currently make her run for the hills. If she was going to be attracted to anyone again—the last thing she'd pick was an eternal bachelor.

He nodded. 'Mainly.' He put a hand on

his chest. 'I treat women well. I just don't go the final distance. And I always try and keep things friendly.' He tapped a few keys, clearly answering one of the messages.

'Doesn't that get a little messy?' She took a bite of her croissant, hating the fact she was getting drawn in.

'Only if you let it,' he said breezily. She was getting a whole new picture of this doctor, and it was...interesting.

'Have they all moved on?'

He nodded as he chewed. 'Most of them.'

'So, you're the one that got away?' she teased.

He blinked, and his face broke into a smile, then he shook his head. 'I hope not. I hope I'm the one that...' he was clearly thinking about it '...prepared them to meet the love of their life.'

'Ahh...' Madison smiled. 'So, they all go on to get engaged or married after they leave you?'

'Quite a few have.'

Her brain was teasing her for being so straightforward with this new doctor that she barely knew. But he seemed to have invited this chat, and she was keen to ease things and have a smooth working relationship between them both.

'Maybe you're just a good luck charm for them.'

He kept smiling. 'Now, that sounds better than *the one that got away*. That's kind of foreboding. Like the kind of guy you see in all those comedy films, and I don't mean the hero.'

Madison could feel herself start to relax a little. This was getting easier than she'd thought it would be. Maybe he'd just written off her snappiness the other day as exactly what it had been, horror and embarrassment. If he had, that was a relief.

'You mean like the one they all either laugh at, or when he's the actual baddie?'

Fletch's eyebrows shot upwards and he laughed. 'Baddie? Love it. Is it Scottish? Or is it just because we work in a world of kids?'

Madison shrugged. 'Bit of both, probably.' She bit the inside of her cheek and then asked, 'So, you see your job in life as to prepare whoever is the current girlfriend for the man who comes after you?'

Fletch had the grace to look a bit sheepish. 'I like women. I do. I like dating. I like having a relationship, I'm just not ready for marriage and families.' He said the words and then cringed, lifting one hand. 'Sorry, I didn't mean it to sound like that.' He took a deep breath. 'I heard about your husband. I'm very sorry.'

Madison wasn't upset. She was used to people saying things around her that some might consider thoughtless. But she'd moved past that. She nodded in acknowledgement. 'Thank you. You might hear people around here mention him. Jason worked in Radiology. The twins were very young when he died, so they don't remember him.' She steadied herself for a second. 'But I have videos, I have photos of us all together, and I have them up around the house. They know about their dad, and they know he died in an accident. I have good support from my hospital colleagues, and from Jason's family—they might be at the other side of the city but they help as much as they can, so we do okay.'

She got the usual sense of awkwardness that she always recognised when she spoke about her bereavement. But it was much better to get this over now, rather than have it as the elephant in the room, with a new workmate. She understood he would already have heard about her circumstances from someone else around here.

She licked her lips and looked out across the cafeteria, being hit by a wave of melancholy. 'Was Jason the love of my life? I'd like to think so.' She gave a soft smile. 'Will I become the female version of the eternal bachelor? Probably not. I'd like to think I'd meet someone else at some point.'

The expression on his face had changed from a bit awkward, to a hint of sympathy. She wasn't sure if she was grateful or offended. 'Do you get lonely?' he asked.

Her skin prickled as if the wind had just blown past them both. The palm of her hand automatically started rubbing up and down one of her arms and she gulped. She was sitting across from a really handsome man. She was trying to make the part of her brain that noticed the colour of his eyes and slight dimple in one cheek switch off.

He'd just told her he was an eternal bachelor and always bailed on a relationship before it got serious. He was the opposite type of partner than she would ever look for—when she ever decided she was ready to do that.

She closed her eyes for a second. 'I get lonely when one of the twins is upset and I can't attend to them both at once. I get lonely late at night when I can't fall asleep and my brain works overtime. I get lonely when the kids are sleeping and I'm lying on the sofa myself watching the TV. I get lonely when one of the kids does something great, that makes my heart swell, and I don't have anyone to share it with.'

She took a thoughtful pause and added, 'But loneliness isn't just for people who are single. Sometimes people in relationships feel lonely too.' She opened her eyes and locked them on his. She could see the surprise on his face, and he must be wishing he hadn't asked the initial question. She wasn't quite sure where all that had come from, it just seemed to bubble up from deep inside. 'I'm lonely when I don't have someone to ask, does my bum look big in this?'

He laughed, and she could feel the small wave of relief from them both. 'Sorry,' she said quietly. 'No one has really asked me that.'

She looked around the cafeteria and he followed her gaze, even though it didn't focus on anyone in particular.

He gave a slow nod. 'I guess most of your colleagues still have you in their head as being Jason's wife.'

She knew he was right. It was natural. 'They do.'

There was silence for a few seconds and she didn't want any more awkwardness to

descend between them. She pushed her coffee cup away. 'Are you finished?'

He nodded, and she wondered if he was
relieved. 'Will we go up and see what we can
do for Adrian?'

She cleared their dishes onto her tray
and stood up, giving a nod. And as he followed her, she tried to make sense of the
deeply personal conversation she'd just had.
She wasn't quite sure why she'd opened up
to Fletch. Maybe it was because he was a
stranger. Maybe it was because he hadn't
known Jason and didn't have memories stuck
in his head. But somehow, she wasn't quite
sure how to make sense of all this.

Fletch was having a strange old day. He was
happy to work steadily with Madison. She
was conscientious and he stepped back to
allow her to assess her patient. As he watched
her every move, he could see how sensitive
she was towards Adrian's mother, who was
clearly anxious. But there was something
else. He could almost feel it in the air. Every
now and then, their gazes connected and
Fletch could swear he felt a buzz. A hint of
something between them. Of course, he ignored it, just as he suspected she was doing.

Because they had a child to focus on. But it was still…there.

Adrian had been booked today as a new patient, with a chronic condition. It was common to see a new child with a chronic condition when they moved into the area. It was important that a child's care was as coordinated as possible. But when Fletch had first met Adrian and his mother this morning, he'd realised that Adrian likely had a chest infection and needed treatment. That was why he'd referred Adrian on to Madison for some specialist physio assistance.

She was professional, and her knowledge and experience shone through. When Adrian's chest film was available, they could see the damage in his lungs and subsequent chest infection. Fletch prescribed IV antibiotics, which the nurses set up and administered. Once they were completed, Madison started her physio. The massage had to be vigorous to help the sticky mucus in Adrian's lungs, but Madison was clearly used to adapting her skills for children and took the lead from Adrian's mother.

Fletch had worked with a whole range of professionals in his life. Most of them skilled and hard-working. But there was something about Madison that drew his attention. Her calm manner, her sweetness. There was something about her aura. He felt a little spellbound seeing in action something he'd definitely never experienced at work. The glimmer of attraction was absolutely there, but he tried his best to push it away. They'd already had that slightly awkward conversation downstairs where he'd declared himself as the eternal bachelor—without revealing the probably imprinted behaviours of his mother. That seemed like a ridiculous excuse now, and he wondered why he'd always chalked his behaviour up to that without examining it any further.

His attraction to Madison struck him as odd. Of course, he'd dated work colleagues in the past. But Madison was a person he'd never date. She had been widowed for only a few years, and had two young kids, her hands were clearly full. It wasn't that he hadn't dated women with children before. He had. But he was conscious of the fact he didn't want to play with children's emotions and become part of their lives when he knew deep down he would walk away. As a kid, he'd liked some of the guys his mum had dated. Some of them had been kind and considerate to him, taken an interest in his academics or sports interests. Then, in a flash, they'd been gone. Fletch had never wanted to do that to a kid.

He was guessing that Madison was either his age, or slightly older. Her brown hair had always been in a ponytail when he'd seen her. She had tiny lines around her eyes, and her skin was pale with a few freckles. He blinked as he realised just how much detail he'd noticed about Madison.

There had been that awkward meeting in the staffroom, where she definitely had been sleeping, and snoring just a little. But he cringed as he remembered how clearly embarrassed and upset she'd been, and wished he'd handled things a bit differently.

Their conversation downstairs earlier had been illuminating, and he got the impression she'd told him things she wouldn't normally say. Maybe he felt responsible now. He'd almost let her admit something that she might have wanted to for a long time.

And the words resonated in his brain. In the blink of an eye, he'd imagined her lying awake at night, and on the sofa. He'd imagined that space in someone's heart when their child did something, and the other parent would never see that.

And even though he knew he shouldn't be having these thoughts, or taking in her shape in her uniform, or how dark brown her eyes were, he knew it was happening.

Once she'd finished with Adrian, he spent some time with the boy's mother, persuading her that Adrian should stay in overnight for some more IV antibiotics.

He moved around the ward, and went down to do an outpatient clinic, enjoying spending time meeting more patients and their families. He would be here for two years—it was important to try and build relationships.

By the time he went back up to the ward later he had a few more patients to see. As he approached the nurses' station to update some charts he could see Madison frowning. One of the nursing staff was clearly relaying a message from the phone to her.

'There's been an accident on the MRT, so they're delayed. They think it will be an hour before they get here.'

The MRT was the Mass Rapid Transit system and was Singapore's railway. It was usually very reliable and this was unusual. Madison glanced at her watch, and he saw her wince. 'What's up?' He couldn't help but ask, even though it was none of his business.

She pressed her lips together, and looked rueful. 'This is a child who lost their leg a few years ago. They are coming for a review of their new prosthesis. There have been issues and I really need time to work with the team to ensure the best fit and make sure there are no balance issues.' She looked up at the main clock on the wall. 'The crèche closes at six. I have to pick the kids up. I can't short-change this family. I need to spend time with them.'

He could see the pain on her face. And he understood. He had patients he would go above and beyond for too. 'They can't reschedule?'

She took a deep breath. 'They are about to go on holiday for six weeks. They're going to Australia and New Zealand—it's their first holiday since the accident and I don't want Hope's mobility to be compromised while she's away.' Madison gave a sigh. 'I want her to have the time of her life.'

'I'll help.' The words were out before he'd even thought about them.

'What?' Her head turned in surprise, and he was conscious of a few other heads turning too.

He shrugged. Help out a colleague, for a professional reason? Of course, he would. 'I have no plans. I can help with the children.'

She blinked and opened her mouth, but the

words didn't come out. He felt a small flare of panic. Maybe she didn't want him to look after her kids?

'I mean, I'm a paediatrician. Of course, I can entertain your children for an hour or two if it will help you out.'

Everyone was looking at him now. 'Madison?' he prompted.

'Thank you,' she said, clearly stunned. Then it was as if her brain kicked into gear. She nodded to the nurse on the phone. 'Let the family know I'll meet them in the rehab suite.' She turned to Fletch. 'Do you mind if we go down so you can meet Mia and Justin? I want them to know that we are...friends. I also need to introduce you to the crèche staff again and let them know I'm happy for you to look after the children.' She bit her lip. 'Where will you take them?'

'Do you have a preference?'

He wondered if she wanted him to bring her children up to the ward area. But she took a breath. 'There's a children's playground in the hospital grounds. How do you feel about that?'

He smiled. 'I can do a children's playground. Point me in the right direction.'

She nodded gratefully.

It didn't take long to organise things. Mia

looked at him with a mix of disinterest and amusement, Justin looked at him with caution. They were still engaged in activities with their crèche workers and Fletch promised to come back at six.

'Are you sure about this?' Madison asked as they walked down the corridor.

'No problem,' he said casually. It didn't feel like a big deal to him. He knew she was widowed. She'd told him her in-laws were on the other side of the city.

She looked a bit hesitant. 'I'm going to head down to the rehab suite and prepare things for my patient. Will I just come to the playground after we finish?'

He pulled his phone from his pocket. 'Better swap numbers just in case I have to move about.'

'Wh-where would you move to?'

He raised his eyebrows. 'You have three-year-olds. We both know that they're going to be in charge. If they need the toilet or some food, I'll do exactly what they tell me to do.'

He saw her tense shoulders relax back down. She pulled out her phone. 'I'm not sure I want to be one of the women in your phone,' she joked.

'Consider it an honorary position,' he countered. 'If I put you in a room with all my exes, I'm sure you'd tell me I had impeccable taste.'

This time it was Madison's eyebrows that rose, but she still swapped numbers with him before hurrying off.

It was almost six before he knew it and he hurried down to the crèche where the staff had Justin and Mia ready and waiting. Both had their jackets and small backpacks on their shoulders. He knelt down. 'Hi, guys, I'm Fletch. Remember?'

There was the smallest of nods of the head. 'So, we're going to the playground to wait for Mummy like she said, okay?'

Both nodded and he held out his hands. Mia slotted her little hand into his without a moment's thought. Justin was more wary. His hand took a few seconds to come up. Fletch led them through the corridors, to the elevators and down to the main entrance. The playground was only a few minutes away.

He asked some questions but only Mia answered. Her speech was clear and to the point. Her sentence construction was good. He couldn't really judge with Justin because he seemed lost in a little world of his own, just padding along beside them.

When they reached the playground, Mia was quick to shrug off her jacket and backpack and dump them on the bench with Fletch before running off to climb the slide. He waited for Justin to do the same. But instead, after he'd taken off his jacket, Justin sat up on the bench alongside Fletch.

'Don't you want to go play?' Fletch asked.

Justin shook his head. Fletch did his best to try and engage him in conversation, conscious that Justin might just be shy. He'd met lots of kids, was well aware they all developed at different paces, and all had individual personalities.

But Justin gave the bare minimum of answers. Fletch could tell that Justin understood him, comprehension didn't seem to be an issue, but even when Mia came over and tugged at his arm to join her, he refused. After a few minutes, he leaned in towards Fletch.

Fletch put his arm around the three-year-old. 'Are you tired, buddy?'

Justin gave a nod and closed his eyes. The climate in Singapore was warm and Justin's skin felt comfortable, so Fletch wasn't concerned he was sick, or had a fever. Some kids did exhaust themselves at day care, and he was just here to keep an eye on them, and make sure they were safe, he shouldn't pry.

Mia had befriended all the other kids in

the playground and was quite the boss, taking charge and telling them what to do even though some were twice her height.

After a while, he pulled Justin up onto his lap, and let him cuddle in against his chest. He sat there, feeling the rise and fall of the small chest against his. It was nice.

During his training, he'd spent many a night shift in the various neonatal units he'd covered in. Fletch had never been averse to letting a small baby sleep against him to let their mother or father have a break. He'd also spent time with kids who'd been sick overnight, and ended up staying with them until they were eventually settled.

He'd always pictured in his head that eventually he would do this, once he was a father. Everything up until that point was just him in training. But before, being a father had seemed so far off. He'd imagined he'd be in his late thirties, maybe married, and working as a consultant in a permanent place. All of a sudden, he realised he wasn't a million miles off any of those things. He was at the start of his thirties, and he'd landed a job he'd really wanted. Two years was something. But he hoped the opportunity could become permanent. The future he'd imagined had started to sneak up on him, and he hadn't even noticed.

He glanced down at Justin again. While he had multiple memories of holding kids through the night, he couldn't recall ever doing this. Being in the daylight was different. He could see people passing, glancing in his direction. Would people assume these were his children?

Mia occasionally came over and dug into her backpack either for some grapes, or for a drink of water. Justin kept sleeping.

He hadn't even realised how much time had passed when his phone chirped. He glanced at the screen.

Where are you guys? Everything okay?

He typed a reply.

Still at the playground. All good.

After a few minutes Madison arrived. She seemed a bit out of breath, as if she'd rushed to get there.

He watched as her eyes instantly found Mia, who waved over from where she was playing on the slide. A frown creased her brow as she sat next to Fletch and instantly put her hand on Justin's forehead, checking his temperature.

'He's been sleeping the whole time,' said Fletch. 'He hasn't played at all. Mia, meantime, is queen of the playground.'

He could see the mixed emotions on Madison's face. She stroked Justin's hair. 'He's been doing this. He seems so tired all the time. But he never sleeps well at night. He's just irritated.'

Now it was Fletch's turn to frown. 'Have you had his bloods checked? Does any kind of anaemia run in the family?'

She sighed, and he was sorry he'd said it, as he could see the guilt flush over her face. 'Not yet,' she said. 'I wonder if he's having a growth spurt. Or, if he's just getting overwhelmed with things at the crèche.'

Their glances locked and he didn't look away. He didn't want to. They might be discussing her child, but there was still something else, something in the air. He was determined not to look away and eventually Madison gave a small sigh and looked down towards her lap.

Fletch knew he had to tread carefully. He barely knew these kids. And Madison was a new colleague. He'd already offended her once. Last thing he wanted to do was do it again. Particularly when he couldn't work out what was going on between them. Was he reading this wrong?

He took a breath. 'Sorry, it's not my place to say anything. But, if you want me to have a look sometime, we can have a chat, and see if we can come up with something.'

It was Fletch's way. Even though he was a paediatric consultant with a wealth of training, he was crucially aware that parents always had to be his partner when it came to kids. Nobody knew their kids better than their caregiver.

She gave him a sideways glance and he could tell she was thinking. After a few moments she gave a nod of her head. 'I'll have a think about it. Sometimes I think that because we see so much in the hospital, it can give us the tendency to blow things out of proportion and imagine worst-case scenarios.' She held up her hands. 'Maybe I just have a kid that's not going to be a good sleeper. It happens.'

He adjusted Justin on his lap. 'You're right. It does. But know, if you want me to have a look, I will.'

She reached over and put her hand on his arm. 'Thanks, I appreciate that.'

He couldn't help but let his eyes go down to where she had her fingers on his skin. He was feeling sensations that he shouldn't be. Not at all. He swallowed as the warm little body against his chest shuffled to get more comfortable.

'No problem,' he mumbled, not making eye contact with her, and immediately feeling stupid.

He lifted his head as she moved her hand away. 'Do you live near here? Do you need a hand getting home?'

He could tell she was instinctively programmed to say no. 'I don't mind,' he added quickly. He stood up, still holding sleeping Justin.

'Do you want me to wake him?'

She shook her head. 'No, don't. He'll just be grumpy.' She looked around. 'Actually, I live about a ten-minute walk from here. Would you mind? The children and I walk in, and back, every day. I've just stopped bringing the double stroller as I thought they were getting too big for it. And it's not the easiest thing to manoeuvre when the streets are busy.' She gestured towards Justin. 'But I hadn't figured on him sleeping.'

Fletch gathered up his things and waited while Madison collected a reluctant Mia, who was still ruling the playground.

The streets of Singapore were busy, with

lots of people who had clearly finished work, and were heading to the many bars or restaurants in the area. The tantalising aromas around them made his stomach growl in anticipation.

People smiled at them as they walked past, probably assuming they were family. Normally, Fletch might have felt a little uncomfortable, but this felt fine.

He instantly straightened his spine a bit more as the feeling settled in his mind. Why wasn't he uncomfortable? Was it because of the thoughts he'd just been having? Or was he really thinking about changing his eternal-bachelor status?

He wasn't dating Madison. That wouldn't happen. They were just friends. So, what was it about this woman that was making him question things? Sure, she was pretty. Sure, she was good at her job. But there was something else, something deep down at the pit of his stomach that made him look at her in a way he knew he'd never looked at anyone else.

He was curious about her husband. Everyone at work spoke highly of him. He hadn't heard a single bad word. He wondered if they'd met at work, or at school. Had Madison dated yet since her husband died? Somehow, he suspected not, not for any reason other than how tired she'd looked the first time they'd met.

'Any plans this weekend?' he asked casually.

'Oh, yes.' She glanced over her shoulder and laughed as they dodged the people on the streets. 'Laundry. Laundry. And laundry. Or, as my gran used to call it "the washing".'

He smiled at the thick accent she dropped into. 'What? No space flight? No cruise ship?'

She signalled they were changing direction and they turned a corner towards a large central apartment block. 'I'll have you know I am the owner of multiple cruise ships and space rockets. Usually, I find them in the middle of the night when I try to visit the bathroom without turning on the lights. My feet have the scars.'

'Ouch.' Fletch winced at the thought of it.

He could tell she was getting more relaxed as they entered the building and she pressed for the elevator. 'You okay with this?'

'Sure,' he agreed as the doors slid open. It only took a few minutes to reach her apartment and as she opened the door, Mia ran on inside. Fletch could see a fairly large apartment with light floors and large windows. And there, on the wall opposite the entranceway, was a photo of Madison and— he guessed—her husband.

It was a snapshot, with Madison looking around ten years younger, and wearing a red dress. Jason had on jeans and a T-shirt, and had his arms wrapped around Madison's waist. They were looking at each other and laughing. Something tugged inside Fletch. They looked happy. As if they had the whole world at their feet.

They had no idea what would happen next.

Madison caught his gaze and gave a small smile and held out her hands for Justin. Her eyes drifted to the photo and there was a flash of sadness as she took Justin. 'I like my kids to see their dad every day,' she murmured. 'I want them to know he'll always love them.'

'Of course,' said Fletch as he tried to swallow the lump that had appeared in his throat.

There was a second of awkward silence. 'Thanks for today,' Madison said quietly.

'No problem. Maybe tomorrow you'll get a chance to tell me about your patient.'

'Sure.' She smiled.

He stepped back as she closed the door. Fletch headed back to the elevator. As he climbed back inside and pressed the button for the ground floor, his eyes were still fixed on her door.

And he couldn't quite say why.

CHAPTER THREE

MADISON HELPED THE young man to his feet and into his crutches. She had a strange role in the hospital, funded by two streams, Paeds and Rehab. But sometimes, like today, she was called to assist in other areas.

A colleague had phoned in sick due to their mother having a fall, and Madison was in the ER, this time helping a young man who'd just had a plaster put on his ankle learn to use his crutches.

She didn't mind this. It did mean she'd end up with a backlog of work for the next few days, but she could cope.

The emergency work just felt like an extension of her rehab role, and she was lucky within rehab she worked with both adults and children. Today had been mainly about assessing people after accidents or breaks to make sure they could go home safely. An eighty-nine-year-old man who'd damaged his knee had nipped up and down a flight of stairs with one crutch like an acrobat, while this teenager was definitely struggling. She took her time, giving him some more instructions, and demonstrating with a different set of crutches until finally she'd been satisfied he was safe to go home.

As she completed her electronic notes she heard a baby crying in one of the nearby cubicles. It was a horrible cry that sent a chill down her spine. Her natural instinct couldn't stop her and she moved over to the cubicle, seeing a pale-faced man clutching the baby.

'Is someone seeing to you?' she asked.

'The nurse has gone to page someone,' he said. She could see his hands shaking. The waves of exhaustion were emanating off him.

'Do you want me to take a turn?' she offered, holding out her hands.

She could tell he was torn. 'This is my sister's baby,' he said. 'Our father is sick, and she went to help. She's only been gone a day. I said I could help as I've looked after Jia many times before. But he's been really upset for the last few hours.'

'Let me help,' she said, taking Jia into her arms and taking a good look at the baby. Her skin chilled. As someone who'd spent a few years working in Paediatrics she had a horrible suspicion of what was wrong with the little one. His temperature was clearly high. She checked the chart the nurse had completed, ten minutes before, then rechecked with the digital ear thermometer again. She marked in the results and peered back out from the cubicle.

She couldn't see the nurse whose name was on the chart, and she wasn't sure which paediatrician was on call today. She didn't want to leave carrying Jia and it was clear his uncle was exhausted. She pulled her phone from her pocket and sent Fletch a text.

Who is on call today? I'm down in the ER and suspect a baby has meningitis.

Madison was well aware she was a physio. Her range of expertise was different from a doctor's and it wasn't for her to diagnose a baby with meningitis. But she'd learned over the years to trust her instincts and to voice them. The people working around any child should be a team, and the worst that could happen here was that she'd be wrong.

The nurse came back and did a quick double take at Madison, then gave a grateful nod. 'The paging system is down. I've phoned up to Paeds but they are looking for the on-call doctor.'

Madison pulled a face, 'I just texted Fletch to ask who was on call.' She was slightly worried the nurse might think she was over-stepping.

'The new doc? Great, thanks. If we don't hear something in five minutes, I might go on up to the unit and grab someone. Would you be okay with that?' she asked Madison.

Madison nodded, knowing if it came to it, she would do that task instead. But a few seconds later, just as Jia's scream was getting more high pitched, Fletch appeared at the cubicle.

'Paging system is down,' he said quickly, 'and I'm not sure if Dr Zhang knows yet. But in the meantime, can I help?'

Both Madison and the nurse nodded at once, and Fletch stepped inside, introducing himself to the uncle and quickly taking a history. He laid Jia down on the trolley and did a quick but thorough examination, his face serious. Madison watched as, even though Jia was upset and screaming, Fletch kept his voice smooth, talking in a steady stream to the little one through the examination, and occasionally stroking his face.

Madison could see his notes.

No rash
High temperature
Colder hands and feet
Irritable
?bulging fontanelle

He asked Jia's uncle a few questions about the baby's feeding and nappies over the last few hours and gave a slow nod of his head.

'We're going to transfer you both upstairs to the paediatric unit. I suspect Jia has meningitis and there's a specific test we need to do. We will also put a small intravenous line in, to give him some antibiotics.' He took a breath. 'Can you call your sister? I would be happy to talk to her.'

Jia's uncle looked stunned and started to shake and cry, moving back over and gathering Jia up in his arms. 'I can stay,' said Madison quickly as she pulled over a chair and put her arm around his shoulders.

She might not be able to do the complicated procedures, but she could free up the nurses and Fletch's time to do what they needed to do to help Jia.

Within a few minutes they all headed up to the paediatric unit. Fletch had spoken to Jia's mum and reassured her of the best possible care. She was on her way back. Madison kept her arm around the uncle, who was starting to calm down now. She'd already told the ER staff where she'd be and that she'd stay to support the family member during the lumbar puncture.

The test could be difficult to perform, and caregivers could frequently be upset during it, so Madison was happy to offer to help.

By the time they were on the ward, the staff there had a bed ready, a trolley with the equipment for the lumbar puncture and another trolley prepared with the intravenous equipment and antibiotics. Madison knew, as soon as the call had been made upstairs, that the staff had gone into automatic pilot, knowing that time was of the essence.

Fletch remained the calmest man in the building. It was the aura he had about him. One of the more junior doctors came to observe and it was clear she was impressed too.

He slid the tiny needle into the base of Jia's spine while he was turned on his side. Madison ended up holding the baby as his uncle was too upset but the procedure was literally over in minutes. Fletch made the decision to start Jia on antibiotics as soon as the sample was sent to the lab and within forty minutes of the baby appearing in the ER, the IV was running.

The nurse who would lead Jia's care signalled to Madison to go and take a break, giving her arm a gentle squeeze. 'Good call. There's something in the breakroom for you and Fletch.'

Madison gave a sigh and a grateful nod. She waited for Fletch to speak to a few colleagues and write up his notes before heading to the staffroom.

The coffee machine was switched on and bubbling and two pieces of hazelnut chocolate cake were sliced and each covered with a napkin. She gave a broad smile. 'Someone's brought birthday cake in.'

Fletch poured coffee into two mugs and brought them over, sitting down beside her.

It had been a few weeks since that day he'd offered to look after the kids for her. Neither had acknowledged it, but it was as if something had changed in the air between them. There was a closeness that Madison wasn't sure she could acknowledge. Of course, they'd seen each other around the hospital in passing. But they hadn't actually sat down together and had a proper conversation, and she didn't want to admit that made her a little sad.

She enjoyed the happy-go-lucky aura Fletch often had about him. It kind of lifted her into another space, where she didn't want to think about sleepless nights, laundry and dishes. But she knew that, right now, what they both needed was a debrief.

She was conscious of how close they both were on the sofa. But it wasn't uncomfortable. It was…reassuring.

'Thanks for the text,' he said, lifting the napkin from the plate.

'Thanks for answering. I wasn't sure who was on call. Just had a feeling about the baby.'

He gave a nod. 'Dr Zhang has put a different system in place while the pagers get fixed. He was on the surgical ward doing a consult, so it's likely I would have come down anyhow.'

'How do you think Jia will do?' she asked nervously.

'I'm almost sure this is bacterial meningitis, and the waiting is always the hardest part now. We've got him before he became septicaemic, but that doesn't mean it won't still happen. The next few hours will be crucial.'

'Do you want me to stay to help with the uncle?'

He looked at her for the longest time. 'You've got the kids to think of,' he said finally. 'And won't you end up with a whole backlog of work?'

The coffee she'd just sipped seemed to stick in her throat. Was he telling her he didn't want her around? Or was it something else?

She questioned the way her brain did this. And it only seemed to do it around Fletch. In other parts of life she took people as she found them, and was confident in herself and her abilities. But with Fletch, his mere presence had her second-guessing herself, in a way she wouldn't with someone else.

His phone sounded and he pulled it out of his pocket. His mood shifting and a smile spreading across his face.

'What is it?' she couldn't help but say, even though it was entirely none of her business. Her brain was still churning away. Maybe his other words had just been genuine concern for a colleague?

'Monique, one of my exes, has texted to say that she's expecting. I'm delighted for her. She always wanted a family, and she and her husband are over the moon.'

Madison thought for a minute. 'Doesn't it ever feel a bit odd that your exes text you stuff like that?'

He looked surprised. 'Not at all. I want

to know she's happy. I want to know she's doing well. Same for all of them. And if any of them were ever in trouble, I'd help in a heartbeat. I think I might do the friend stuff better than I do the boyfriend stuff,' he said, then give a bit of a worried shrug as if he was thinking about all this.

7He looked up and met her gaze, the shrug continued and he pulled a face. 'I've gone to a few weddings, too.'

'Really?' She couldn't help but almost laugh. 'And the grooms don't mind?' She took a bite of the hazelnut and chocolate cake.

He honestly looked surprised. 'Not that I've noticed.'

She shook her head. 'If Jason had wanted to invite one of his exes to our wedding, I'd have had questions.'

'But why?' He looked genuinely intrigued. 'All my exes have moved on. We're still friends, they are getting married, and they invite friends. Why is that wrong?'

Madison gave a shudder. 'It just seems… odd.'

He raised his eyebrows. 'My choices are odd? Maybe it's you. Did you finish with previous boyfriends with screaming and fire?'

She was thoughtful for a moment. 'Only

one, but he cheated and that's different. The others…' Her voice trailed off and then she shuddered again. 'Some of them were bad choices in my teenage years or early twenties, and I might actually cross the street rather than be forced to say hello again.'

He laughed and ate more cake. 'That says more about you and bad choices.'

She knew he was teasing her.

'With the exception of your husband, of course,' he added quickly.

Those words kind of killed the humour in the room.

Madison pushed away the remainder of her cake and settled back in the sofa with her coffee, her shoulder brushing against Fletch's.

'I don't think you'll like this one either,' he murmured.

She turned her head, suddenly conscious of how close they were, and pulled back a little. 'What's the this one?'

'I'm godfather to one of their babies.'

She groaned.

He put his hand on his chest. 'And I don't want to blow my own trumpet, but I am the best godfather on the planet. Sonny is cute and cheeky, and will likely cause his parents a world of trouble. It just shines out of him.

And I get to sit on the sidelines and be the all-knowing uncle.'

'What age is he?'

'Nine.' He shook his head. 'Just wait till those teenage years hit. I'll likely end up with him staying at mine for a bit. Viv has already threatened me with it.'

There was still lightness in his tone, but she caught something else. 'And you'd do it if she asked?'

He didn't hesitate. 'Absolutely.'

Madison set down her coffee cup and folded her arms. 'That's kind of nice. And exactly what someone who wasn't a full-time parent would say.'

He grinned. 'You've been talking to Viv, haven't you?'

She smiled too. 'Not yet. But we think the same way.'

He held up both hands. 'Hey, I just want to be everyone's friend. Is that a bad thing?' He shifted a little and then continued. 'I sometimes feel bad about ending things. I never want to give false expectations, but, you know, I still sometimes feel like I'm letting someone down. So, I do my best to end things well and stay friends. It's important to me, because I—' he held up his hands

'—I like these women. They are good people. And I wish them well.'

Madison's stomach clenched. What was it about being around this guy that made her brain whirr, her skin tingle and her mouth sometimes say things she shouldn't?

'What happens when you decide you want more?'

His hands stayed in mid-air, sort of frozen, before descending slowly. He took a slow breath. 'I guess I've just not reached that stage in my life yet,' he said carefully.

Madison put her elbow on her knee, resting her chin on her hand. 'What happens if you reach that stage in your life and realise that one of your exes is likely the person you were supposed to live your life with?'

The expression on Fletch's face changed. For a moment, he was thoughtful. 'I have to be honest, I don't think that's likely to happen.'

'You won't ever meet the love of your life?' She couldn't hide her cynicism.

He shook his head. 'No, that I've met her yet. That I've let her slip away.' He took a few seconds. 'All my exes were lovely people—all very different and unique in their own way.' He put his hand on his chest. 'And I think if you had a realistic conversation with any of them, they'd say the same as me. It just didn't click. We had fun, we liked each other, we respected each other. I know that I loved some of them. But would that love have lasted for ever?' He was already shaking his head. 'I don't think so. Because I don't think I've met her yet.'

'Met who?' It was a silly question, but she was kind of mesmerised and disappointed by his words right now.

'My person,' he said without pause.

Their eyes locked. Madison's insides were not designed to twist and turn like this. He hadn't met his person. That was what his brain said.

And the ridiculous tiny voice in the back of her head was chanting, *But he has met you. You didn't even get considered.*

Honestly, was she some kind of teenager all over again? Where had that ridiculous thought even come from?

Seconds passed, and their gazes remained connected. He licked his lips and she had to tell herself not to lean forward. He'd said the words. He hadn't met his person yet. She just couldn't look away. And, apparently, neither could he.

But her brain wanted a different answer.

One where she was at least considered—even for the briefest of milliseconds.

'Do you think you'll know right away?' she said, her words almost a whisper, still looking into those eyes.

His eyes were green. Pale green. That somehow looked good with his dark hair. She'd noticed them before, had tried not to look too closely. But from this position, it was impossible to miss.

His reply was throaty. 'I'm not sure. Should it be love at first sight? I'm not sure I believe in that. Do I believe in getting to know someone first?' He licked his lips. 'I guess I do.'

'I guess that means your person could be right around the corner,' she said, before she could stop herself.

'Or ten years away,' he countered.

Her skin chilled and she breathed, forcing her mouth into a smile. 'Or ten years away,' she repeated.

She shifted her position on the sofa, wishing she hadn't eaten that cake, and telling herself that was what was playing havoc with her insides.

'I guess I should get back to work,' she said, lifting her plate and cup and carrying them over to the sink. 'If you don't need any help, I'll go back to the ER to cover.' She turned towards the door.

Fletch moved next to her, bringing his own plate and mug. She thought he was going to just agree and let them part company, but his words stopped her footsteps.

'When did you know?' There was an intensity in his eyes.

She spun back, 'What?'

'Your person. When did you know that Jason was your person?'

Madison bit her lip. It was an intensely personal question, but one she'd likely brought on herself. 'I knew within a few weeks of dating. We clicked. And everything else around us clicked. We both got jobs here. We found an apartment that we liked, things seemed to move quickly—but it didn't feel quick. It felt right.' She took a breath as she felt a tug at her heart. 'And I just knew.' The lump in her throat was real and she blinked back tears, spinning back around and walking out of the door before there were any more questions.

Guilt swamped her. She'd been sitting there, having different thoughts, stupid thoughts, about a guy she hardly knew, and who had helped her out once. He'd given her no real sign or indication that he gave her a passing thought. But even though she'd tried to fight it, and ignore it, she knew that he was stirring something in her that she hadn't felt in a long time.

Part of her was horrified. This wasn't Fletch's issue. This was hers. Maybe she was just reaching that stage—the one where she might consider moving on, trying to meet someone else. But even as the thought fully formed in her brain, she still felt weighed down with guilt. What if people thought three years wasn't long enough?

She didn't even know if it was. She just knew for the first time in for ever she was attracted to someone again. There. She'd admitted it.

She laughed bitterly as she walked down the corridor as she tried to tug her untidy hair back into a ponytail again. She wasn't young. She wasn't thin. She wasn't pretty. She had twins. Would any man ever find her attractive?

Even if she wanted to think about moving on, she had so much more to consider. Her in-laws. Her own parents. Her workmates, and the most important people of all. The twins. How might they feel if she met someone, and decided it was time to introduce them to the twins? The last thing she would ever want was to have a line of perpetual boyfriends who would meet the children, decide this relationship wasn't for them, and walk away.

She could never do that. She could never line her kids up for any kind of hurt. Why was she even considering any of this?

It was too much hassle. Too complicated. She finally smoothed her hair down and rewrapped the ponytail band, taking a few breaths.

No. She would stop these thoughts. She would stop them right now.

Fletch would be pushed to the back of her thoughts completely.

She had to guard her children, and her heart.

Fletch was back on the ward, focusing on Jia. He'd prescribed some pain relief for the baby as well as the antibiotics, and between Jia's uncle holding him, and his lead nurse rocking him on her shoulder, Jia finally seemed less agitated. The lab phoned after checking the cerebrospinal fluid, confirming it was bacterial meningitis, which reassured him around not delaying commencing the antibiotics.

All the time he kept working his brain kept going back to one person. Madison.

He couldn't understand it. He'd met lots of women in his life. But for some reason, at this place, he'd met someone who he'd had one of the biggest conversations in his life with.

She put him on the spot. Held him to account in a way that was challenging, uncomfortable and definitely attractive.

She wasn't his type. He kept telling himself that. But his curiosity about this woman just grew and grew. He found himself looking for her, and drawn to her.

When she'd asked the question about his person, he'd been thrown. Lots of people had joked with Fletch that he would meet someone, settle down and have a couple of kids, and, truth be told, he'd always thought that would be in his distant plans.

He'd never felt ready before. He'd never had reason to be. Because he'd never met the person that conjured up this amount of feelings in him. This amount of turmoil. This amount of concern, and curiosity. But now, here he was, looking into a colleague's dark brown eyes and wondering if he could kiss her.

It was strange, the buzz he felt between

them. He wasn't entirely sure that it was all just in his head. If it was, then thank goodness no one could hear his thoughts. But if it wasn't, and Madison recognised the buzz too, what then?

Did he really want to test a relationship with someone who was widowed and had two young kids to take care of? It would be like no relationship he'd ever had before, and Fletch wasn't entirely sure he was unselfish enough to be that person.

The thoughts made him uncomfortable. If he couldn't be honest with himself, how could he hope to succeed in a relationship with someone else?

'Dr Fletcher, can you come and review a few patients, please?' It was one of the other staff and he immediately nodded and went to do his job.

Paediatrics had always been his thing. From the second he'd started working as a doctor, he'd known where his speciality would be. Others were obsessed with different kinds of surgery, or specific medical conditions. Fletch had known it would be Paediatrics. From that first moment he'd stepped onto a paediatric ward he could feel it in his blood. The chaos. The innocence. The beauty. He'd just gelled with the area as his speciality. And he hadn't changed his mind, not for a single second.

Children were honest. Children wore their hearts on their sleeves. And some of them didn't have the best start in life—through no fault of their own. Babies and toddlers often couldn't say what was wrong, and Fletch saw that as his job to find out.

He'd worked in several countries now. But Singapore had drawn him back. The healthcare system was better than in some other countries. The climate was good, life expectancy was good here too. For him, as a medic, job opportunities were good. Although the population was dense, he'd never felt crowded. He'd mastered some of the Malay language, and a smattering of Indian, which, alongside English, meant he could communicate with the majority of the people he came across. His contract was for two years. But, even before getting here, Fletch had been considering the fact he might want to stay.

It wasn't that he never wanted to work in the US again. He'd trained in Chicago and been brought up in the mid-west. But as a boy, he'd always wanted to travel the world. He'd worked in Germany, France, Australia and now back in Singapore for the second time.

His thoughts drifted back to Madison. She was Scottish, but was still here. It sounded as if she'd also decided to make Singapore her home in her early twenties. He couldn't help but notice the parallels in their lives that pulled them back here.

He wondered if she eventually might want to go home to Scotland where her parents were. He'd never commented on the fact she might need support, and he never would. Apparently, Jason's family helped her. Would they still help if Madison moved on and met someone else?

He gave himself a shake. Again, none of his business. Why did most of his thoughts focus on Madison?

He took a breath. Was he imagining that something was in the air between them? Was Madison the most beautiful woman in every room? Probably not. But she was the only woman that held his attention. He liked that her hair occasionally fell out of place. He liked the fact she offered to help with most situations, and had a real commitment to her work and her patients. He also admired the way she coped with her children on her own, alongside handling whatever was going on with Justin.

He could see a number of Madison's traits in Mia. The determination, and the leadership. Clearly, he hadn't known Jason, but he was sure he must be in there too.

Fletch wasn't sure what to do next. He felt as if this whole thing were like an elephant in the room. Was he brave enough to take the next step when he didn't know what on earth he was doing?

He kept asking himself the question as he worked for the rest of day, wishing someone would whisper the solution into his head.

CHAPTER FOUR

HE'D GONE FOR an early morning run, trying to sort his head out. He had run in Singapore previously, but this time his route took him mysteriously past both Madison's apartment and the hospital. He was approaching the entranceway to St David's when he caught sight of a familiar figure stretching a little way in front of him.

'Madison?'

She looked up, her hair in a ponytail on top of her head that obstructed her view. She flicked the hair away. For a second he wondered if she was embarrassed. After all, the black and red running clothes left nothing to the imagination. But then, his were much the same.

She straightened up. 'I didn't know you went running,' she said in surprise.

'Same.' He smiled. 'How did you manage to get away?'

She blinked, then must have realised he was talking about the kids. 'Oh, twice a week I drop them into the nursery then come for a run before I start work. It's the only way I can fit it in.'

He glanced at his watch. 'How about breakfast before we start the day?'

There was a café right on the street next to him, and he saw her give a quick glance, bite her lip, then say, 'Sure. That would be nice.'

Fletch thanked the fact he had his debit card tucked into his waistband as they sat down at one of the outside tables. The waitress was out instantly taking their order.

The coffee appeared quickly and Madison took a sip and gave a long sigh. She glanced around. 'This is nice. Mornings are usually top speed for me. Taking a few minutes out is nice.'

Fletch smiled in agreement. It *was* nice to be able to take a breath. He could only imagine her normal morning routine—and that was before she hit work.

'Before you ask,' he said, 'I've already checked on Jia before I headed for my run. He's been stable overnight.'

'Good.' She nodded.

She relaxed back into her chair. And he found himself leaning towards her. 'So—not work—something else, if you had a whole day off, what would you do?'

Her brow crinkled in amusement. 'Okay, I'm assuming I'm not taking Justin and Mia with me?'

For a second, he wondered if he'd offended her. But Madison didn't look offended. She just smiled. 'I'd read a book, have a bath, go for a massage, lie in the park in the sun, maybe take in a movie, or get my hair done.'

She met his gaze and laughed. 'What? Too much? Or just said it all too quickly?'

He laughed. 'Well, you didn't need to think about that for long.'

She smiled in agreement. 'I know.' She blew a few strands of hair out of her face. 'I love my kids dearly, they are the best thing that ever happened to me. But do I want some me time on occasion? Of course, I do. I'd be a fool if I didn't admit that.'

He liked that about her. She was honest. But she did it in a half-joking way. He didn't doubt for a second she loved her kids, but now she was striking his interest even more.

Her black T-shirt and black and red running leggings hugged every part of her. Madison wasn't stick-thin, like an athlete, she had curves. Ones he could notice and admire. But Fletch had never really been a guy solely attracted by looks; he was always drawn to a person. And even though he'd barely arrived in Singapore, it seemed that he'd already found someone who captured his attention.

As the waitress set down their breakfast dishes, and Madison started on her scrambled eggs, he started chatting again. 'Okay then, what book and what movie?'

She bit into some toast and thought for a few seconds. 'See, you probably think I'm going to say something like *Pride and Prejudice*, but nope, not for me. I want some sci-fi. Giant planet worlds, technology I've not even thought of, and an anti-hero like Darth Vader.'

He almost choked. 'You don't want much, do you?'

'You shouldn't ask questions if you don't like the answers,' she joked.

And just like that he knew. He knew at some point he'd like to ask this woman out.

It was too soon. He didn't know enough about her. She didn't know enough about him. But he was certainly keen to find out more.

'Who says I don't like the answers? Maybe I'm just a bit surprised. Go on, then, what's the movie?'

She shrugged. 'Depends entirely on my

mood.' She gave him a mischievous glance.
'I'm a sucker for a Christmas film. But I
swing between *White Christmas* and *Die
Hard*. And I absolutely adore action movies. Fast cars, burning buildings, chases, ex-
plosions, space battles.'

'You're like every guy's dream date, then,
aren't you?' he said before he had time to
stop himself.

She raised her eyebrows and let out a
laugh. 'Not sure I've ever been called that
but—' she glanced at her watch '—for half
seven on a Tuesday morning, I'll take it!'

He liked that she was neither offended nor
shocked. His eyes were drawn to her clear
skin and bright smile. Madison Koh was definitely pretty. But the biggest attraction was
her easy manner. He wondered how he would
feel if he were in her shoes—a single parent, widowed, with twins and full-time job.
Would he be able to cope as well as she apparently did, and still make the time to have
breakfast with a new colleague?

He could tiptoe around things. Try and
find out if she was dating again—or if that
was a possibility. Or he could just ask. But
would that seem too forward?

They finished breakfast and both looked at
their watches at the same time. 'No rest for

the wicked,' said Madison brightly. 'I need to jump in the shower and get along to the ward.'

'Me too,' he agreed. 'But thanks for joining me for breakfast. It was...' he couldn't hide his broad smile '...nice.'

She shot him a cheeky glance. 'Nice? Wow. I'm bowled over with compliments here.' She gave him a wave. 'Gotta run, see you later.'

And she did run—or jog—over to the hospital and disappear inside the main entrance. He did his best not to fixate on her figure, but failed miserably. His spirits were high. New job. New colleagues. New possibilities.

CHAPTER FIVE

FLETCH FINISHED HIS last set of notes and started walking through the hospital. Checking the ER, the rehab ward, and then hanging about the crèche. Madison appeared, rushing as usual, then her footsteps faltered as soon as she saw him.

'Something wrong with Jia?' she asked instantly.

He shook his head, and glanced over his shoulder. 'No, he's doing good. I thought we should talk.'

Madison looked confused, a frown creased her brow and he wondered if he was about to make the biggest fool of himself. 'About what?' she asked.

'Us,' he said without hesitation, figuring if he was going to make an idiot of himself, he might just do it straight away.

Her face straightened and he saw her taking a big gulp. 'Wh-what do you mean?'

'I feel as if you're stuck somewhere in my brain. I can't explain it. I can't make sense of it. And I figured I'd just ask you if I was going crazy, or if there is something in the air between us. I might be imagining this. And just tell me, and I'll go off into a corner and hide. I promise, I'll be entirely professional and won't mention any of this again.' He stopped babbling, and tried to read her face. She looked stunned, and he hoped that wasn't because he'd just blindsided her with a whole heap of nonsense. 'Just tell me. Am I imagining things? Because it doesn't make sense.'

She blew out some air through her lips and set her bag on the floor, glancing towards the door of the crèche. There was no one else around. They were entirely alone.

'You're not imagining it,' she said. 'And I can't explain it either. I like you,' she said, and he could tell it took real bravery to say those words. 'But I don't know if I'm ready to like you,' she added, her voice a bit shaky.

He took a step closer, putting his hand on the sleeve of her jacket. 'Have you dated anyone since Jason died?' he asked, wondering if this was the road he should take.

She gave a sorry smile. 'I've been on one

kind of date, that I didn't tell anyone about, and it didn't work out. I wasn't ready.'

'How long ago was that?'

'Two months,' she said with no hesitation.

There was silence between them for a few moments and Madison rested her head against the wall. 'You're a serial dater, Fletch. The actual opposite of the kind of guy I would look to date.'

He nodded. 'Oh, I know. And maybe this will earn me a slap, but I never figured I'd want to date someone who was a widow, with twins.'

He could see her hold her breath, and he wondered if he'd been too honest.

'You told me yourself you walk away if anything feels like it could be serious. I don't want to introduce my kids to someone who might only be in their lives for a few months. I'm not comfortable with that.'

She moved as another member of staff came down the corridor to collect their kids from the crèche. And he was conscious that she didn't really want other staff members to see them together.

'Okay,' he said carefully. 'So, do we ignore this? Pretend neither of us noticed and just get on with things? Do we avoid each other, or smile and play nice?' He shook his head.

'I've never been here before. I've never been attracted to a woman and not asked her out.' He gave a small laugh. 'But I've certainly never had the same conversations that I've had with you.'

'Ditto,' she said, and he looked up and caught her gaze. Those brown eyes again. Something sparked in her. 'You haven't actually asked me out.' Her lips turned upwards into a smile. 'Not that I'm nitpicking.'

And in that second, he just knew.

'Madison Koh, would you go on a date with me?'

She licked her lips and spoke quietly. 'I think you and I should set some ground rules.'

He nodded in agreement. 'Okay.'

'Don't be offended. But I'd rather keep this between ourselves.'

It wasn't the first thing he'd expected her to say, and he was a bit surprised. 'Okay, why?'

She held out her hands. 'I feel confused enough. Lots of the people around here knew Jason and were his friends. I'm not sure how the general news that I'm dating again will go down with some of them.'

'And it would be entirely none of their business,' said Fletch promptly.

She gave a rueful nod. 'And I know that.' She put her hand on her chest. 'But if I don't know how I feel about this, and if I'm ready or not, the last thing I want is everyone else wading in with their opinion.'

'So, you want to keep things secret?' He wasn't sure that he liked that, but he understood where she was coming from. Did he want to end up with a reputation as the hospital love rat who maybe broke a widow's heart?

Madison was looking at him intently. '*I* want to know how I feel. If I'm ready. If I can cope with dating again.' She paused and gulped. 'If I can feel again.' Her voice was shaky.

'You're scaring me, Maddie,' he said. 'We might go on a few dates, realise we're not a match, and have to give this up.'

She straightened her shoulders. 'Or, we might go on a few dates, decide that things between us are good, and then I can watch you run for the hills. I'm sticking my neck out here, Fletch. I feel as if all the risks are on my side. All I'm asking is that we keep things quiet for a while.'

He realised she was right. This was a much bigger deal for her than for him.

'But how can we work this out if you don't

want me around the kids? Are you comfortable asking Jason's family to babysit if you're going on dates again? Do you know how they would react?'

She winced. 'I haven't had that conversation with them yet. But I know it will need to happen. To be honest, I think they might be all right. They take the twins overnight every second weekend—just for one night, and they generally juggle between when we are all working. They've done it since Justin and Mia were just over a year and I'd stopped breastfeeding. It's mainly been to give me a break and to give them some alone time with their grandkids. They really do dote on them.'

'So, that will work out as one date every two weeks?' he asked. He couldn't help but raise his eyebrows.

She gave him a smug smile. 'Maybe it's going to teach you to take things nice and slow. Get to know each other, so we can decide if the spark is real, or if we're just bouncing off each other.'

The eyebrows stayed up. 'Bouncing off each other.' He laughed and shook his head. 'You've no idea, the pictures in my head right now.'

'Stop it.' She gave him a strong nudge.

'So, what do you want to do? Dinner? Sightseeing? Movie?'

She leaned against the wall again. 'I haven't been to the pictures since before I was pregnant. But I'm not sure that's first on the list for me.'

'The pictures?' He was amused.

'That's what they call it in Scotland. I like it.'

'So, why didn't you go when you were pregnant?'

'Duh…because I didn't fit in the chair.' She laughed. 'And I was too uncomfortable, right from the beginning. So, it just wasn't a good idea. I have missed it,' she said thoughtfully. 'But no. Somehow, I don't think sitting in the dark for three hours, and in silence, will be the date of my dreams.'

'I'm moving up to the date of your dreams?' He smiled in pleasure, 'Pressure's on, then.'

She shook her head. 'Don't get cocky. No one likes a smart-arse.'

He grinned. 'So, when is our first date? When are the kids with their grandparents again?'

'Saturday,' she said. 'Two days.'

'So, I've got two days to plan the dream date?'

Her face broke into a smile, and for the first time she looked relaxed around him again. Something fizzed inside him. They were doing this. They were actually going to go on a date.

'So, we're on. Saturday. What time will I pick you up?'

She gave a smile. 'How about lunch time?' He didn't want to second-guess but he could swear that smile reached her eyes.

'Pick you up at one-thirty,' he said, and walked back down the corridor trying not to do a skip in his steps.

CHAPTER SIX

SLEEPLESS NIGHTS WERE a great leveller.

As Justin fretted on and off, Madison's brain worked overtime. Maybe she should just ask Fletch to have a look at him. She'd searched the Internet for everything, which didn't help, because all she came up with were tragic stories of some unheard-of disease or another.

Madison also didn't want to seem like either a helicopter parent, or a paranoid wreck. As a professional, she was used to dealing with both kinds of parent. The nurses on the ward joked that as their kids had all grown older, they'd all been bitter about the lack of sick days they'd managed to achieve throughout their school years. Nurses were quick to assess, and several admitted to being called by the school when their child—who'd felt a bit squeamish—had actually vomited at school.

As she lay on the sofa, with Justin sprawled across her, she spotted a red notebook that she'd picked up from a stall at the hospital advertising new kinds of pharmacy drugs. It was small enough to fit in her uniform pocket. Ideal. She'd start writing down Justin's symptoms, and even her panicky thoughts. It might help her put some context around things so she could decide if she wanted to ask Fletch to examine him or not.

The trouble was, it wasn't just Justin that was on her mind. Part of her was glad she'd had that honest conversation with Fletch before they'd considered moving forward.

She couldn't pretend she wasn't attracted to him, or deny there was a spark between them. But there were so many other influencing factors.

He wasn't her kind of guy. He wasn't. She'd never been the type to date the hospital Lothario. Her Jason would never have been labelled that way. Honest, fun, and with integrity was how he was best remembered.

And even though Fletch had numerous ex-girlfriends, she'd noticed things about him. He hadn't said a single bad word about anyone that he'd dated. The fact he'd remained friends with so many—and that was still a sticking point—surely showed that he'd treated these women with respect?

He'd seemed genuine when he said he wanted them all to be happy. But he'd also been honest with them all about not being ready to settle down.

And this was the part that made her stick the most.

She'd known him a month. A month at arm's length. How on earth could she know if he was the kind of person she might consider having a longer-term relationship with, or spending time around her kids?

Red flags were waving at the side of her eye right now.

Maybe he would just want to date for a few months and then let it come to a natural end. She hadn't properly dated since Jason had died. Could she cope with that? That feeling of rejection, and possibly a broken heart?

Justin squirmed in her arms and she moved like a contortionist trying to get back up from the sofa and take him through to his bed.

There was no way she was having a broken heart. She was smart enough for this. As soon as feelings started to get involved rather than naked attraction, she would reassess things.

The underlying question was still there—was she ready?

She moved over to the window to stare out over the night view of Singapore. Hotels and tower blocks were everywhere, with tiny lights in windows illuminating the dark sky. It made her feel so tiny in this world. One small person in a place with more than five million.

Madison rested her head against the cool glass. She knew what Jason would say, and what he would have wanted for her. He would have wanted her to be happy, just as she would have wanted the same for him had things been turned around.

She was lonely. She could admit it. She would love some adult company. A hand on her waist or round her shoulders. Lips at her ear, or on her neck. Fun, sexy texts. Someone to lie next to in bed and have ridiculous late-night conversations with.

She shivered and lifted her head. Yes, she was ready. Even if Fletch wasn't the right person, he was a good start. At some point she had to get back out there. Her work colleagues had to stop thinking of her as part of a pair, and start to see her as a living, breathing woman, who might want to date again.

It was time to set her life in motion again.

Yes, Fletch might be a heartbreaker. But he was an honest heartbreaker. She knew what she was getting into. And he did too. Because she'd told him she wasn't sure about all this. At the very least, the man with a thousand exes could teach her how to date again.

She gave a small laugh to herself as she glanced at her sleeping children and walked back through to her own bedroom. Her wardrobe doors were open and for a moment she wondered what on earth she would wear for her date on Saturday. And then she started laughing again, the warm feeling spreading through her. Because Madison Koh couldn't remember the last time she'd thought about what to wear.

She might buy something new. Shoes used to be her thing. She'd loved stilettos and high heels. At the moment, they were only ever pulled out of the cupboard by Mia and Justin, who tried to totter around in them. Most were bashed beyond all recognition and she didn't mind that for a second.

But maybe it was time for a new pair. And a few other new things.

Life had been too busy for her to take time to focus on herself. She hadn't let herself slow down at all, in her haste to get back to normal life and create a new routine for herself and her children once Jason had died.

It would be nice to take a breath. To have some space.

As she climbed into bed and pulled the duvet over her, her thoughts had finally started to settle. The immediate panic was gone. This might be a good decision—if she let it be.

Fletch had spent the last few days imagining every date known to exist in Singapore. He wanted to do something special. He wanted to have time where he and Madison could chat, flirt, be comfortable around each other, and just enjoy each other's company.

He still didn't know enough about her. And he wanted to.

But he was so, so conscious that he had to tread carefully.

This wasn't like any of his previous relationships. He couldn't compare this to any of the women he'd casually dated. Everything about this was unusual for him, and the confidence he usually felt around women had dimmed. He wanted to get things right.

He reached her apartment right on time and she swung the door open before he even had a chance to knock.

'Wow,' was all he could say.

Madison was ready. Her hair was loose around her shoulders, she had on a red dress, belted at the waist, and a pair of red stiletto heels.

'Double wow,' he said, with a wide smile, pointing at her shoes.

She looked down. 'What?'

It was that second that he noticed her lipstick matched her dress and shoes. He took back previous thoughts. Madison was quite possibly the most beautiful, sassy and spectacular woman he'd ever seen.

'I like the shoes,' he started, then paused. 'No, I *love* the shoes. But we might be doing a bit of walking today.'

She stared him straight in the eye, clearly contemplating telling him she could walk a thousand miles in those shoes. And he would have believed her.

She had a slim tan bag over her shoulder and she bent down, took her shoes off and flung them in the bag. 'Hold this,' she said, disappearing back into her apartment and coming back with a pair of black Converse boots on her feet.

She pulled the apartment door closed and spun around, her hair brushing his nose and a waft of spicy amber and orange aroma hitting his senses. 'Just so we're clear,' she said, 'at some point today, I get to wear those shoes.'

'Your wish is my command,' he agreed. 'I for one will be very happy to see you in those shoes. But in the meantime, let's go.'

Fletch wasn't entirely sure what she'd think of his plans. He just hoped she wouldn't be disappointed. It didn't take them long to reach their destination.

As the green grass sprawled out before them she looked at him curiously. 'We're going to the Botanic Gardens?'

He nodded. 'When was the last time you came here?'

She wrinkled her nose. 'With Mia and Justin's playgroup, while they were still babies. I tried baby yoga lessons too, they were at the gardens.'

His heart sank a little and he ignored it. 'So, the last few times you were at the gardens you were with the kids.'

She nodded.

He reached over and took her hand in his. 'So, this time, you're here as an adult. Our mission—if you choose to accept it…' he winked at her '…is to have a chance to wander and talk. We'll go see the orchids too—as long as you're not allergic and haven't told me.'

The edges of her lips turned upwards. 'I'm not allergic. And the orchid gardens will be lovely. It's a long time since I've been in there.' She gave him a nudge. 'And don't sell me short. We have to walk to the band-stand and take a moment to look at the view around.'

'And probably spoil five or six people's iconic camera shot?' he teased.

She shrugged. 'There's enough minutes in the day for us all.'

They stopped for coffee at one of the cafés near the park entrance, and Fletch took her hand back in his. She didn't object, and he gave her a smile as they started to stroll along one of the paths.

'So, your outfit. You knocked it out the park and put me to shame.' He glanced down at his white button-down short-sleeved shirt and khaki shorts. He looked appreciatively at the red dress again. 'Is it new?'

She gave a little tug at the belt with her hand holding the coffee. 'It is. When you asked me out, I realised it had been a long time since I'd bought something nice, you know, not just functional.' She narrowed her gaze. 'But you've ruined the shoe effect. I used to wear high heels all the time. Loved them. Could have run in them. Hurdled.

Climbed a mountain. But I hadn't bought a pair since before I was pregnant, and the ones I have, the kids just play in them now. So, there was something kind of nice about buying a new pair.' She raised her eyebrows. 'And there was no doubt—no matter what colour the dress had been—the shoes would have had to be red.'

He laughed. 'Even if the dress was orange or pink?'

She threw back her head and laughed. 'Of course! You're so out of date, Fletch. Pink and red, or orange and red, it's a thing now.'

He shook his head. 'So, shoes is your thing, then?'

She took a breath before she spoke. 'They were. And I'd like them to be again. There hasn't been a lot of me time. And I get that,' she said quickly. 'That's the same for every parent.' She sighed. 'Is it wrong that sometimes I'd just like time to breathe?'

He gave her a thoughtful glance. 'An old friend of mine was a health visitor in England—kind of like a family health nurse in other parts of the world. Because she visited babies and children up to five, she thought when she had her own, she'd be fine.' He gave a rueful smile and said, 'She phoned me one night around dinner time as she'd had to put her two-year-old in his room, and was sitting on the floor holding the door handle.'

'Was he having the terrible twos and wrecking the place? I remember those days well.'

Fletch nodded. 'Oh, he was having the terrible twos—but he wasn't wrecking the place. She'd put him in his room because she said she was ready to kill him.'

Madison closed her eyes. 'I think every parent has had that moment at some point. It's awful. You feel so helpless—as if you're doing the worst job in the world.' She looked at him with interest. 'What did you do?'

'I told her to keep talking. So, she did. She sat on the floor and let it all out.' He shrugged. 'I knew the little guy was safe, and I could hear him through the door. His tantrum was spectacular. But having an adult chat to tell her she wasn't a bad parent, and literally no one has this down, seemed to help her.'

She gave him a suspicious stare. 'But you're not a parent. How do you get it?'

'Who says I do? I try to. That's what's important. Especially as a doctor. You know we both see things we have to question and we have to ensure every child is safe, but we also know that most parents do a good job, even against challenging circumstances. I try to always remember that.'

He swallowed, realising he might be getting too close to the truth for Madison. She'd been practically alone these last three years, there would have been lots of times she probably felt like pulling her hair out.

'How is your friend now?' she asked.

'Kelly's good and decided the terrible twos weren't so terrible after all. She's expecting again.'

While a smile appeared on Madison's face something flickered behind it. Was that a hint of sadness?

He moved on quickly. 'So, tell me, did you always want to be a physio?'

She laughed. 'Not at all. I kind of fell into it. I was one of those kids who finished school, taking very generic subjects because she wasn't sure what subject she wanted to apply for at university.'

'So, you just picked physio out of thin air?'

'Yes, and no. I went to some of the university open days. I looked at a variety of English courses, some computing, I flirted with the thought of working in film, but eventually met a woman who was manning one of the stands, she worked as a physio and explained her role, the science behind it, and how it often helped people regain their independence. I'd never really thought about the role before and it intrigued me.'

'And that was it? Four years later you qualified as a physio?'

'Yes, and the more I did the course and the placements, the more I loved it. It's the perfect job for me.' She turned her head towards him. 'What about you? A straight-A student and a walk right in to medicine?'

He pulled a face. 'Yes, and no. Yes, to the straight-A student. No, to walking right in. I had to wait two years. My father—who was also a doctor—had a stroke. Like most people it was right out of the blue and totally unexpected. He was fit, not overweight, no blood-pressure issues, but he'd had some strange viral infection that year, and it seemed to do some lasting damage to his systems.'

'So, you deferred your studies?'

'Yes. Dad needed a lot of assistance to begin with, but he started a rehab programme that really worked for him. It was slow, with small gains. He still doesn't have full use of his right arm, but for the most part, he's done well.'

'Did he get back to work?'

'He works a couple of days a week now, and seems to get on well.'

'You must have done a bit of physio yourself, then, if you were helping your dad with his programme?'

'Yeah, I did. I think it gave me the chance to appreciate the part everyone plays in a team—before I even started medical training.'

She smiled at him. 'Thank goodness.'

He looked amused though. 'You considered film?'

'Absolutely. Not to be an actress or anything like that, but to work behind the scenes. Never happened though and that's probably for the best. Who knows where I might have ended up?'

The park was tranquil, even if it was in one of the most populated cities in the world. There were plenty of other people strolling along the winding paths and letting the summer air surround them.

They reached the turnstiles for the National Orchid Garden and Fletch paid the small fee to get in. As soon as they crossed through, they were treated to the enchanting aroma of the variety of lilies. Colours were everywhere. Vibrant displays for red, pink, purple and white, each part leading into another that was even more spectacular.

'It's so beautiful, but I feel as if I should whisper,' said Madison. 'There's something so peaceful about this place.'

'It is peaceful,' Fletch agreed. As they wound through the paths, some parts were overshadowed with greenery and others in the brilliant sunshine. The climate in Singapore was perfect for the growth of the huge variety of specimens in front of them. 'One thousand types,' he murmured, 'and over two thousand in this garden alone. It's no wonder people get lost in here.'

She wrinkled her nose. 'I'm not sure I took you for a gardening type.'

'I'm not really. Dad had a greenhouse. It became quite central during his rehabilitation.' He gave her a wink. 'I can grow you a nice tomato, or green pea.'

'Hidden talents,' she joked. 'Don't let that bit of gossip get around the hospital. You'll be fighting them off.'

'I'm taken,' he said, without hesitation.

They'd moved past the fountain, the mist garden and walked through a dozen arches of multicoloured orchids by this point. She stopped walking and let her hand drop from his. 'This is our first outing. And we agreed we'd keep a low profile.'

He looked at her curiously. 'We did, and we will. But I don't date more than one person at a time. Do you?'

The words were like a challenge. 'Of course, I don't,' she said aghast. 'You know I've not dated for years. Can you let me get the hang of this again?'

'Oh, you can get the hang of it again, as long as you don't break the dating rules.'

He'd started walking again and she slowly joined him as they made their way out of the orchid garden, back into the main park and towards one of the cafés.

'What are the dating rules?' she immediately asked.

He couldn't help teasing. He wanted her to be relaxed around him. He understood dating again was a big deal and, while that also intimidated him, he was trying not to think of what it all could mean.

'The dating rules are simple. Always food in one form or another. Honesty as much as possible. Alternate picks for movie nights. No bad music, and...' he paused '...dancing at every opportunity.'

Madison's mouth fell half open. 'What?'

He pulled her into his arms and waltzed

her around in a few circles. Her eyes were wide. But her body moved in tune with his. Her footsteps faltered and she laughed, looking down at her red dress and Converse boots. 'Shouldn't I have changed shoes for this?'

'You can if you want, but we might still have some walking to do.'

'Why, where are we heading next?'

'This is for amateurs. Let's show the world we're professionals.'

Her nose wrinkled but he could tell she was intrigued.

He still had one hand at her waist and his other in her hand, keeping her in the waltz position. Their bodies were only inches apart, noses only a little further. No one was bothering them. Fletch could notice a few glances in their directions.

He could kiss her. Right now, he could kiss her. But they were supposed to be taking things slow. And even though she was right in front of him wearing a gorgeous, figure-hugging dress, the scent of her perfume catching his senses, her red lips still only a few millimetres from his... 'Come,' he said. 'Let's go to the place you made me promise I'd take you.'

It only took them ten minutes to reach the

bandstand. The octagonal gazebo was surrounded by terraced flower beds, palms and a ring of yellow rain trees.

Madison's face lit up. 'There's no one there.' Her footsteps quickened. He understood her haste. The bandstand was rarely empty. It was one of the most popular photo spots in the whole park. It was also a renowned wedding photography spot, but fortunately it was late afternoon at this point, and most of the wedding pictures had likely been done.

He held her hand as he led her up the steps, and gave her a bow. 'Want to put your shoes on now?'

The converse were toed off and she opened her backpack to pull out her red shoes. It only took a second for her to slip them on and stand in front of him. 'You were saying?' she teased.

He held out his hand. 'Do you want some music?'

She was laughing as she slid her hand into his. 'I'm terrified to let you choose.'

'How about we play a game of chance? I'll put my phone on random and we'll dance to the first song that plays.'

She tilted her head as she thought about it.

'Give me a tiny clue of what's on there before I agree.'

He pretended to have to think about exactly what was on his phone. 'Some hard rock, some soul, some oldies, a few from the charts in the last few years, and some film soundtracks. Oh, and the odd Christmas album.'

She laughed out loud. 'So, it really is a lottery? We could be dancing to "I Wish It Could Be Christmas Every Day" in the middle of summer?'

'Shouldn't life be full of random chances?' He wanted to lean forward and push her hair away from her face. It was blowing in the wind, and blocking his view of those hypnotic brown eyes. She licked her red lips and he almost groaned at the world for playing with his body, mind and levels of testosterone.

'Go for it,' she joked.

He paused for a second to press a button on his phone then slid it into his back pocket. He didn't wait for fate to thwart him, and just took her into his arms again and started moving as the music started to surround them.

Both of them burst out laughing at the same time as Berlin's 'Take My Breath Away' started playing.

Fletch couldn't hide his delight and picked her up and swung her round.

'It's a fix.' She laughed as he set her back down and they began swaying against each other.

'I told you I had old movie tunes in there. It just so happened that someone was clearly smiling down on us today.'

'It is an old one,' she agreed. 'I wasn't even born when the original movie came out.'

'Neither was I.' He grinned. 'But we've both still seen it, and know the song. Isn't it weird how some things just last the test of time?'

He'd meant the words in an entirely different context, but wanted to bite them back as soon as he saw the fleeting emotion in her eyes. But she didn't fold to the feelings. She just dipped her head for a second, gave a tiny shudder and lifted her head to meet his gaze again.

In that tiny movement, he suddenly realised just how brave Madison Koh was.

He felt it.

And he also felt a bit terrified.

The last thing he wanted to do was lead this woman on a merry dance—metaphorically speaking, of course.

This wasn't normal for him. He couldn't

remember *ever* feeling like this. That had to account for the terror. And the other overwhelming thought was that, right now, he didn't want to be anywhere else in the world but right here. With her.

He ignored the small lump that had definitely appeared in the back of his throat and just let her body move gently against his. 'I've got you,' he said.

Nothing more. And he meant it. He'd wondered if he—and this—would end up just being part of her journey of moving on and moving forward. He couldn't push himself to think long term yet. But what he also knew was that he was in exactly the place he wanted to be.

She gave him the smallest smile and he could feel the tension release from her muscles. He allowed himself to relax too, and smile at the music and dance their way around the bandstand.

He noticed a few people snapping pictures of them, and even though they were from a distance, he was conscious that sometimes people posted on social media spontaneously. He moved them, so that Madison's back was to the people. The last thing he wanted was a member of Jason's family or someone from the hospital seeing a private moment between them.

The music came to an end and he gave her a little bow, not drawing her attention to what he had noticed.

'Thank you for the dance.'

She turned and picked up her bag. 'Thank you for finally letting me put my shoes on. I bought them specially. Do you know how mad I'd have been if I hadn't had a chance to show them off?'

Fletch put his hand to his chest. 'As a guy with the odd female friend, I can safely say that's definitely not something I want to find out.'

She put the bag at her shoulder. 'The day is still young. What's next?'

He grinned. 'You know how I told you one of the dating rules involved food?'

She nodded and he could tell she was interested. 'I definitely like dating rules that revolve around food. I know it's only around five, but I have a favourite place that means we need to jump on the MRT. Are you up for it?'

She patted her stomach. 'I'm always up for some food. Lead the way.'

He took her hand again and they headed out to the nearby station, Fletch swiped for tickets at the machine and they jumped on the next train. The journey was pleasant. MRT was one of the most efficient transport systems, it had a reputation for being clean, safe and even had built-in Wi-Fi for those doing longer commutes. They exited at Downtown station and took the five-minute walk to Lau Pa Sat market.

Even this early in the evening the delicious smells and noise of crackling food pulled them in.

Her eyes were gleaming. 'I wondered where your favourite place was.' She looked around the busy marketplace. 'But which is your favourite seller?'

'I'm already hungry with just the smells,' Fletch admitted. 'But the best satay stalls won't be set up yet. How do you feel about a drink?'

The air was warm and Madison pulled at her dress. 'A drink would be good.'

'What do you normally drink?'

She wrinkled her brow. 'Usually wine, or a cocktail.' Then she laughed. 'I say that as if I have managed to find time to have a drink in the last few years. I think I can count on one hand how many I've actually had.' Her eyes kept drifting over the various beverage places around them. One of them caught her attention. 'How about a craft beer?'

Fletch couldn't help but let the biggest grin appear on his face. 'Sounds like heaven.'

They walked over and perused the beers before finally selecting one each and taking their tall glasses with the chilled beer and having a seat at one of the nearby tables. It was nice just chilling. 'I love people-watching.' Madison sighed, taking a sip of her beer.

'Do you ever make up stories about the people you watch?'

She shook her head and looked amused. 'What do you mean?'

'I had an auntie, and she used to try and entertain me when we were waiting in line for something or were out shopping, by making up stories about the people around us.'

'Like what?'

Fletch scanned the people around them, thinking hard. 'Okay. See that man in the orange shirt?'

Madison saw him instantly. He wasn't hard to miss. Fletch leaned his elbows on the table. 'So, people won't realise, but that's his *lucky* shirt. He wore it to his first date with his latest girlfriend, he wore it to a job interview to get a job he really wanted, and—' he leaned forward conspiratorially '—and he's just about to buy a lottery ticket today, and guess what?'

She put her chin on her hand as she grinned at him. 'He wins?'

Fletch threw up his hands. 'He wins! Now, it's your turn.'

Madison tapped her other hand on the table and surveyed the crowds. It took her a few moments to pick someone. 'Okay, the older woman in the black skirt, beige shirt, with the hat and the pink bag.'

Fletch spent a few seconds before he spotted her. 'Okay, unusual bag colour, but carry on.'

Madison raised her eyebrows and looked mockingly serious. 'This is where it gets dark.'

Fletch started to laugh. He just couldn't help it. 'Okay, then.'

Madison licked her lips. 'So, this lady is not happy. She's found out her lover has been cheating on her. But this woman is no fool. She's like a modern-day Locusta—you know the professional poisoner of Ancient Rome? So, she's found a new untraceable poison and has laced it through his hair products, face cream and toothpaste. She's just left his luxury penthouse knowing that the next time she goes back, he'll likely be on the floor.'

Fletch opened his mouth. 'I'm shocked. Where did that come from? You seem like such a good-hearted person.' He was shaking his head as he started laughing.

Madison was laughing too. 'What did you expect, a fairy-princess story? Because that's not me. Oh, no. I want the thriller, the mystery film or novel. The twisty plot with some characters having a spirit as black as coal.' She threw up her hands. 'That's when all the fun happens.'

Fletch took a long, slow sip of his beer. 'Shocked,' he said as he set it down. 'Shocked, I am.'

She leaned forward. 'Come on, let's do another.'

'You're scaring me now.'

She scanned again and nodded in the direction of a young woman, in a school uniform. She looked in her late teens. 'The other thing I like is some dark academia. So, this is Nora. Everyone thinks she's the school good girl. But Nora is *not* a good girl.' Another teenager, almost identical, emerged from the store that 'Nora' was standing outside. 'Here's where it gets interesting.' Madison beamed. 'That's Jules. Her best friend. But Jules has just won a scholarship to Oxford in England. Nora came second. So, they are just about to go on a school trip to Japan. And at Shibuya Crossing—the busiest crossing in the world—Jules doesn't know it, but she's about to meet a sticky end.'

Madison lifted her beer glass and clinked it against his. 'Cheers.' She sat back in her chair. 'I could do this storytelling stuff all day.'

He leaned back in wonder and kept shaking his head. 'Please tell me this is not the kind of storytelling you do with your kids.'

She pulled a face. 'Not yet. But I suspect Mia might inherit some of her mother's tendencies. She loves attacking her play people with dinosaurs right now, and there are several heads and limbs missing.'

He couldn't help the low belly laugh. 'And you're proud, aren't you?' He held up his beer glass so she could clink it again.

She leaned forward and the clink resounded as she said the words, 'Immensely.'

Fletch leaned back and gave her an admiring glance. Madison Koh was one of the most interesting women he'd ever met. He was glad he'd trusted his gut. Even though his brain had tried to interfere, he couldn't pretend he wasn't interested in her, or deny that he thought she was gorgeous and sexy.

Vibes were there for a reason.

They didn't need to be a perfect match. It didn't need to be the perfect time. He just wanted a chance to see where this might go. And just as he'd realised as he'd been holding her, he'd never felt like this before—he also realised he'd never been prepared to take a chance like this either.

Of course, he couldn't say things would work out. He didn't know that. How could he? Because deep down, he still had doubts. These feelings were new to him. He still wanted to tread with caution.

He leaned across the table and threaded his fingers through hers. 'Are we going to do this all night?'

She gave him an astute look. 'Maybe,' she said decisively. 'Or at least until you can buy me the best chicken satay in the whole of Singapore.'

'Ah,' he said with interest. 'So, it's chicken satay that you want?'

'Doesn't everyone?'

He waggled his hand. 'I'm torn. There are also the prawn noodles.'

'Hmm…' said Madison, clearly contemplating the option. Then she shook her head. 'No. It's got to be the chicken satay.'

They moved along to her favourite stall and watched as the vendor freshly cooked two portions of chicken satay and loaded the steaming food into bowls for them both. They moved to the nearby tables and sat down to eat. Madison gave a grateful sigh. 'This is lovely,' she said. 'Most nights I have to concentrate on having a routine and getting the kids down. Can't tell you the last time I managed to get here after seven when the stalls were open.'

This time, instead of beer, Fletch grabbed them both bubble tea on Madison's instructions and sipped at the unusual concoction dubiously.

'It's more popular here than cola now,' she said, as she watched him.

He screwed up his nose. 'It's a bit sweet for me. But interesting.'

She grinned as she kept her gaze on him. 'You hate it, don't you?'

He pulled a face. 'Kinda…'

'Go get something else.' He didn't need to be told twice and came back moments later with a diet cola.

Madison finished her satay slowly, clearly savouring every bite, before lifting her hands above her head and stretching like a cat who'd just woken up.

'This has been lovely, thank you,' she said as she smiled and looked at the busy streets round about her. 'Makes me feel like I actually have a bit of a life again.'

He was about to ask her a question but she shook her head and lifted one hand. 'Don't take that the wrong way. I love my kids. I love being their parent. But now and then, it's nice to be an adult again. And get to do adult things and have adult company.'

It took her a few moments to realise what she'd said. Fletch had already started laughing as her cheeks flushed. 'Oh, no.' She groaned and put her head down on the table. 'You know what I mean.'

They'd both finished now and Fletch stood up, extending his hand out towards her. 'I know what you mean,' he said genuinely.

She slid her hand into his and they walked back through the bustling crowds to the MRT. 'Want to do something else?' he asked. 'Want to go to a bar, or have you changed your mind, and want to find a film to watch?'

She shook her head and, in that moment, they strode into the stream of red and yellow lights from a nearby store. The lights reflected off Madison's loose brown hair and red dress, leaving him momentarily transfixed at the effect. It was like watching a movie star on the big screen. He didn't need to go to a cinema. He had his own right here.

She realised the lights were illuminating her and lifted her hands, giving a laugh. 'Ten seconds of stardom.'

He moved in front of her, joining her in the stream, and slid his arms around her waist, his face just above hers. 'Maybe it's just giving us the perfect moment.'

He wasn't asking the question out loud, but there was no doubt the question was there. They had been casually tactile with each other all day. He wasn't going to kiss her without knowing it was what she wanted.

He wondered if she would pause, if she would step back, but he didn't have time to process those thoughts before she'd wrapped her arms around his neck and her lips were on his. At first it was the gentlest of brushes. But a few seconds later, the kiss was warm, tender, open-mouthed and inviting.

One of his hands slid up from her waist and into her hair, the silky strands falling through his fingers. The press of her body against his, and the sweet smell of her perfume, mixed with all the scents and noises around them. The world kept moving. But they stayed fixed in place.

For the first time since he'd been with Madison, his brain didn't allow for any second-guessing. This moment, this kiss, was meant to be. He believed that.

As they finally broke apart, he could feel the warm breath from her mouth landing on his cheek. 'Wow,' she whispered.

'Wow,' he repeated. He couldn't stop the broad smile on his face.

She reached up and touched his cheek. 'This has been a great day,' she said, her fingertips pressing lightly. He knew the but was coming. And it did. 'But it's time for me to go home.'

He could argue about how early it was. He could make a case for them spending the next few hours together. He could make a case of what exactly they could spend the next few hours doing. But he got the silent message. For now, this was as far as Madison was prepared to go. And he accepted that.

He gave a nod of his head, not letting himself speak. Again, he took her hand in his and they walked to the MRT, jumping on the next train and heading back to Madison's district.

Of course, he wanted to walk her to the door. Of course, he would have loved to have gone back inside her apartment with her. But once they entered the main doors to her building she turned and kissed his cheek. 'Thank you, Fletch,' she said softly.

He stepped back. She turned and headed to the elevator and he waited until she'd stepped inside and turned back to face him.

'Till the next time,' she said with a smile, and as the doors slid closed he tried to pretend his heart wasn't secretly exploding with delight.

CHAPTER SEVEN

MADISON HAD FLOATED back up to her apartment and the smile had remained on her face while she dressed for bed and took off her make-up.

She hadn't really expected things to go so well. She hadn't really expected to feel so connected to the man she thought couldn't possibly be a match for her.

Was her judgement off? Had it been so long since she'd trod this path that her senses had died and tucked themselves off in a drawer somewhere?

At numerous points today her skin had tingled. Usually when their gazes had connected and she'd felt just…something. Her new dress and shoes were back in the wardrobe. But she could see them. They were half taunting her. Her dress had wrinkles at the waist due to wear, and the shoes had a tiny scuff.

It was almost as if they were sending her a message. *You did this.*

Madison wasn't some teenage girl. She couldn't possibly put a whole lot of stock in one good date. But she could keep it. She could keep the memory of it, and of that first kiss.

She was ashamed to admit she couldn't remember the first time Jason and she had kissed. She was sure she had known previously, but somehow it now just seemed mixed up in her head. It was a distant, hazy memory, whereas tonight's kiss was standing bright and under the spotlight.

She wrapped her arms around herself and smiled. She wasn't sorry to have called an end to the night. She knew what could have happened. It could very easily have happened.

But she wanted to take charge of the pace of things between them. It was easy to get swept away. Whatever happened, she had to work with Fletch for the next few years. It was important she didn't jump in too quickly.

As she sat on the sofa, her long blinds pulled back to let her gaze over the city, her fingers caught the soft notebook on the table beside her.

That brought her back to reality. Justin.

She was getting more and more worried. Vague things. No real, specific shout-out-loud-this-kid-needs-to-be-taken-to-the-doctor kind of things. She definitely couldn't put her finger on it. But something had changed in her little boy. She knew it in every fibre of her being.

She'd doubted herself before. But the last few days, she'd been noting things down. Every little thing.

She was well aware some people might think this was the diary of a hypochondriac mother. But the right person would listen to her, and take this seriously.

And all of a sudden, Madison had confidence in who the right person was. She picked up the notebook, flicked through, grabbed her pen, and started writing again.

'I've added someone onto your list,' said the secretary.

'No problem,' said Fletch as he reviewed some results. 'Who is it?'

The secretary looked over. 'It's the kid of one of the staff members. They asked if they could have an initial appointment to see you and discuss some concerns.'

He nodded. It was always a compliment

when a colleague asked him to see one of their kids and he was happy to do it, conscious that in another ten years, he might want them to repay the compliment.

He didn't even glance at the name, so when Madison walked into his office a few hours later with Justin in her arms he could have—quite literally—fallen over.

His eyes automatically went to the screen. Sure enough, Justin Koh was in this appointment.

He walked around the table automatically, holding his arms out towards them both. 'Maddie? You don't need an appointment to ask me to see Justin. I'll see him any time. Hey, little guy.' He put his face down nearer to Justin and spoke to him directly. 'How are you doing? Remember me? I'm Fletch. One of your mummy's friends.'

Fletch didn't often wear a white coat. He preferred wearing normal clothes when dealing with children. So, he was frequently on the floor during consultations in order to assess a child properly.

Maddie seemed nervous. 'No, I know. But I wanted to make an appointment. I wanted this to be official.' She sat down in the chair opposite his, and arranged Justin on her lap.

'I wanted to discuss some things I've noticed with Justin.'

Fletch could tell she wanted to keep things formal, so he went with the flow. 'Tell me what you've noticed.'

She pulled a red notebook from her pocket. 'So, in the last four weeks I've noticed some changes in Justin.'

'Okay.' Fletch nodded. He always paid attention to what a parent told him. He was also well aware that for some children their stage of development sometimes alerted parents to things that might have been there, right from the start.

'In the last four weeks, Justin has seemed unnaturally tired. At first, I thought it was a growth spurt. But his growth has been steady. Nothing to really draw any attention. And even though he's always tired, he doesn't sleep well at night. I've tried a whole host of different things, without any real success.' She gave a sigh. 'And, of course, I know the two are connected, but I've also noticed other things.'

Fletch was watching carefully. Justin was three. At three, most kids were attention-seeking. Happy to chat, wanting to be involved in whatever was going on. Curiosity would have brought many three-year-olds out of their mother's lap by now, and either exploring the box of toys in the room, or starting to touch all the things on Fletch's desk.

Justin was sitting. Clearly paying attention, but his eyelids did look a bit heavy.

'There are other random things. Sometimes he feels a bit sick and doesn't eat well—even when it's his favourite food. His concentration seems to be affected. Jigsaws he was completing a few weeks ago, now get flung to the floor in frustration. Now and then we get some outbursts, and he gets frustrated with Mia, and they fight. He's also had one or two dizzy spells. And he complains at night that his legs are sore.' Her voice started to crack and she automatically started rubbing Justin's back. 'It seems like a whole lot of nothing that I can't put my finger on. But I just know that there *is* something. And I feel a fool because this is my boy, and I can't work it out. I can't tell him what's wrong and make him feel better again.'

Fletch gave a slow nod. 'Madison, I'm going to help you with this. This could be easy, or it could be hard. We might have to do a whole host of tests to rule things out first, before we consider real possibilities. Are you okay with this?'

Her chin was trembling but she nodded. He pointed over to the examination trolley. 'Okay, so we start simple. Justin, Mummy's going to help you take off your T-shirt and trousers and I'm going to have a little look at you.'

Justin frowned but didn't seem annoyed. He let Maddie slip off his T-shirt and trousers, and sat up on the examination couch with her at one side and Fletch at the other.

A proper top-to-toe physical examination was crucial in assessing children. Fletch was glad that Justin wasn't actively unwell right now with a fever. That always made things worse. And while Justin glared at Fletch the whole time, he let him look in his ears, eyes, nose and throat, and sound his back and chest. He also didn't object when Fletch got him to stand straight to check his legs, spine, posture and muscle groups.

After about ten minutes, Fletch made a few notes and touched Madison's hand. 'Okay, nothing obvious. But I think you knew that. How do you feel about a urine specimen, a nose swab, and, if we put some numbing cream on his arm, some bloods?'

Madison flinched and pressed her lips together. She must have known this was coming, but she gave a nod and said, 'Can Roki do the bloods?'

'Absolutely,' Fletch agreed, knowing that Roki was one of the best phlebotomists on the unit. He handed her a specimen bottle. 'I'll go and speak to Roki while you try and persuade Justin to do a pee for us.'

An hour later, a much more disgruntled Justin was sipping a carton of orange juice and nibbing on a biscuit. The urine dipstick had been negative, but both the sample and the throat swab had been sent to the lab for analysis. The bloods had been expertly taken by Roki and would likely be back in a few hours.

Fletch sat down next to Madison. 'This is only the first few steps. Let's have a look at the overall picture, then sit down again and see if we can narrow down specifics.'

As the process had continued, he'd seen her get more tense, and he got it. She'd vocalised her fears that there could be something wrong with her child. That was terrifying enough.

Madison gave a tight nod and Fletch couldn't help himself. He reached over and squeezed her hand. 'We'll work this out.'

Right now, Fletch was unsure what could

be wrong with Justin, but there was a whole host of possibilities that he would consider. He wanted Madison to have a little faith.

'Will we agree a time tomorrow to look at test results? You don't need to bring Justin. We'll look at what comes back and decide a plan.'

She nodded her head as she picked up Justin again. 'Okay, thanks, Fletch. Come on, gorgeous, let's get back to nursery.'

She disappeared out of the door and Fletch bit his lip.

He was glad she trusted him enough as a doctor to bring Justin to see him. He wished she'd had a chat with him beforehand, but maybe she'd been worried he might say no? Fletch would never have done that, but he couldn't help but wonder why she hadn't mentioned it.

This also muddied the waters between them. Before, they were purely colleagues. Now, she was officially the mother of one of his patients. If things continued to develop between them, depending on the results of the tests, it might reach a point that he'd have to hand Justin's care over to someone else.

Some others might rightly badge this as a conflict of interest.

But Fletch didn't think they were at that point yet. He'd know if they were. At least he hoped he would…

Madison's chest was tight as she delivered Justin back to the crèche and ducked into the nearby ladies to let the tears she'd been holding in flow unhindered behind a bathroom door.

She was shaking, even though she knew it wasn't rational. She'd said the words out loud and got a doctor to see her son. But she hadn't got any doctor—she'd asked Fletch.

His face had been shocked when she'd walked in. Part of her had hoped the secretary would have warned him, when she'd agreed to put Justin on the schedule this morning. But, for whatever reason, Fletch had clearly not realised Justin was on his list.

He'd been gracious and professional, and she was thankful for that.

But in the meantime, she had a whole lot of worry about what could be wrong with her little boy. She texted one of her friends, and contemplated phoning her mum back in Scotland. But if she told anyone else, she would likely only worry them too—and Madison didn't want to do that.

She wiped her face and blew her nose before coming out of the stall and washing her hands, not even bothering to glance at her own reflection. She still had a few patients to see before she finished tonight and wanted to get back to business.

Fletch stared at the swab result, urine results and blood levels, which told him very little at all. A small rise that could indicate an inflammatory response somewhere, or a start of an infection, but nothing major.

Madison appeared in the doorway looking jittery. He called her over and showed her the results on the screen. She was smart enough to understand them without much explanation and he could sense her wave of disappointment. He'd wanted to text her last night, or call her, but wasn't sure if that was an intrusion when he knew there was so much else going on in her life.

She sagged down in frustration next to him. 'Nothing really,' she said with a wave of her hand.

He nodded in agreement. 'Okay, I have a suggestion, but I'm not sure if you'll like it.'

Her brow creased and she looked at him. 'What?'

'I'd like to spend more time around Justin.'

She froze. He could see it in the tensing of

her muscles and the way her mouth formed a small 'o'. 'What exactly do you mean?'

'I'd like to see what he's like at home, what he's like when it's bedtime, how he settles—or doesn't.'

'Y-you don't believe what I've told you?'

He put his hand over hers. 'I absolutely believe what you've told me. But I need something else to work on. I could ask if we could admit him for a few days—'

'No.' The word was out of her mouth instantly.

He acknowledged it, and continued, 'Or, I can spend more time around him. In the park. In my office if you prefer. In the crèche—which I will probably do. But I also think seeing him in his own environment will probably be for the best.'

She swallowed and he could see her contemplating things. 'Would you do this for someone else's child?'

He thought about this honestly. 'Yes, and no. I've done this before when I sensed a diagnosis in a child was going to be tough.'

'Were you dating that mother?' was the rapid-fire question.

'No,' was his honest response.

He waited a moment then continued. 'I respect that you said you don't really want your children to meet someone you are dating. This is complicated. Physical examination was unremarkable for Justin, and his tests haven't specified anything for us. I want to get a better sense of him. I want to see the interactions with Mia, and if that influences him in any way. I want to see how he functions in his own world, his own safe place, rather than in a doctor's office or crèche with other children.'

He watched her breathe deeply. 'I understand what you're saying. I think you could be right. But what does this mean for us? I want there to be clear lines when it comes to my children. I don't want things to be blurred, and I don't see how this is anything *but* blurry.'

'Do you want us to draw a line under things? Do you want to forget about dating?' He was saying the words out loud because he thought he should—it was the respectable thing to do—but his heart was currently held in an invisible clamp.

'No.' Her answer was swift, and the clamp miraculously realised its tension.

Her hand went to her hair and she started fumbling with it, redoing her ponytail, which was absolutely fine.

He waited a moment and then spoke. 'Neither do I.'

She dropped her hands and met his gaze.

'So, how do we do this, Madison?'

'Come tonight,' she said, and he got the impression she was saying this before she changed her mind. 'Bring takeout. The kids like chicken noodles. You can watch him at dinner, see them play together and then you watch as I do their bedtime routine.'

Her movements were clearly unconscious, but she straightened her spine and dropped her tense shoulders. It was clear she'd made up her mind.

'What time?' he asked.

'Early—six p.m.?'

'How are you going to explain the fact I'm there?'

'Friend from work,' she said quickly. 'I'll tell the kids we have work things to talk about when they go to bed.'

He nodded. It was a sensible solution. It made sense. Even if he didn't want it to. Something panged deep down in his belly. This wasn't how he'd expected to feel. Never, in his eternal bachelor days, had he ever really wanted to ingratiate himself into the life of his girlfriend's children—particularly after one date!

He wasn't sure if he was more surprised or conflicted. Of course, he should know his own mind. And his mind right now was quite fixated on Madison. But she was a package deal. And that had to play a part in every move that he made. So, even though he was scared, and his brain screamed caution, he still wanted to pursue this.

'No problem, I'll see you then.'

Madison wasn't sure she'd made the right decision. Her brain had gone back and forth all day, and when she'd finally picked the kids up from the crèche she'd almost texted Fletch to cancel. But things got away from her. Justin was more cranky than usual, and Mia seemed to have had new batteries inserted and talked nineteen to the dozen. By the time she'd wrestled them out of day care, got home, dumped their stuff and finally stripped off her uniform it was almost exactly six.

She pulled back her wardrobe door and stared at her clothes. A green blouse, a pair of black jeans—or the black T-shirt with the sequin lightning flash? But no. She stopped herself, not wanting to draw any attention to what was about to happen. She grabbed the grey yoga pants she normally wore around the house and pulled on an old rock-band T-shirt. Fletch would just have to take her as he found her.

'Guys,' she said, as she steered them into the bathroom to wash their hands. 'Mum's work friend is bringing us dinner. He'll be here soon, so wash up.'

Mia, never one to miss anything, started asking questions. 'Is it Rui? What's she bringing? Is it ice cream?'

Madison sighed but smiled. 'No, it's not Rui. It's Fletch, the new doctor. He's bringing chicken noodles.'

'Ooh...' said Mia and jumped up at the table, obviously ready to start eating.

The knock at the door was perfect timing. Justin still looked mopey, but moved over to the table as Madison went to answer the door.

Fletch had the food in his hands and gave her a nod, looking down to her legs. For a second she thought he was looking at the yoga pants, then she remembered he was more likely looking for the children.

She pulled the door open. 'Come in.'

He stepped inside and his footsteps faltered as he clearly caught sight of the children sitting at the table. Both of them had lifted their knife and fork in preparation for the food.

'Under pressure,' murmured Fletch and started humming the Queen tune as he made his way over to her kitchen. 'How do you want to do this? Put it all out at once?'

Madison opened the boxes, looked inside and inhaled deeply. 'Mmm...' She picked up one and took it over to the table and divided the contents between Mia's and Justin's bowls. 'Here we go, guys.'

She then found two large plates and opened the second container and divided between herself and Fletch. She nodded her head to the right. 'Bathroom's through there. Go and wash up and I'll get us some cutlery.'

She poured some soda for them and water for the kids and Fletch joined her at the table a few minutes later. 'Guys, you've met him before, but this is Dr Fletch.'

Mia was already eating. She chewed for a few seconds then looked at him as only a three-year-old could. 'Red or pink?'

'Pink,' he said without blinking.

'Puppies or kittens?'

'Puppies.'

'You lose!' declared Mia happily.

Fletch gave a look of fake horror. 'How did I lose? How can puppies ever be the wrong answer?'

'Because we're not allowed a puppy in

here. We could only have a kitten—but Mummy doesn't want one.'

Mia side-eyed her mother, and Madison did her best to act as if she didn't notice.

She nudged Fletch and turned her attention to Justin. 'How are the noodles, honey?'

He was stirring them around his bowl, occasionally spearing a bit of chicken. 'Fine,' he mumbled.

Madison breathed. Maybe there was nothing wrong with Justin at all. Maybe he'd just aged into a teenager overnight, and the tiredness, lack of attention and one-word answers were just something she should get used to.

But Fletch seamlessly took over. 'I brought some dinosaurs with me. Do you both like dinosaurs?'

Two little heads looked at him, their attention instantly on him. 'Yes,' said Mia immediately.

'Yes,' said Justin in a low voice.

'Well, once we've finished dinner, and if it's okay with your mummy, I'll give you them.'

Two pairs of eyes turned on her. 'It's fine,' she said quickly.

Fletch was an easy dinner companion, and Madison ate the chicken noodles even though her stomach seemed to be somersaulting around. She was conscious of everything. Every glance, every look. Every time Justin yawned. Every time he was a bit distracted. Then she made herself stop.

She had to stop. She wasn't examining every little move or word of Mia. If she did, she would be exhausted.

Fletch asked both an easy stream of questions. Mia was fascinated with Fletch's accent, and tried to imitate it, making them all laugh.

Once Madison had cleared the dishes, she took out two wine glasses and poured some pinot grigio, handing one to Fletch as they sat down on the sofa. Fletch handed over his bag of goodies to the kids and the two settled on the floor in front of Madison and Fletch to play. Justin disappeared for a few moments and came back with a kit bag that was already full of dinosaurs, which he added to the rest.

Madison wondered how she was supposed to feel about all this. Having Fletch in her apartment and around the kids wasn't nearly as awkward as she'd feared it might have been.

She wondered why she'd built it up so much in her head. She knew the reason he was here. It was to assess Justin. And she could sense he was doing just that. They had the large-screen TV on in the background. It was playing an old nineties film and the children were completely ignoring it as they were definitely in dinosaur land. Petty fights and squabbles were happening as Mia tried to commandeer most of the new pieces, and Justin's little chin jutted out as he held his own against his sister.

He was moving position, occasionally rubbing his joints in a way a child shouldn't. After a while he started rubbing his eyes and getting snarly with his sister. Madison glanced at the clock. It was around forty-five minutes before she would normally get them ready for bed.

'I'm going to switch the shower on. Justin, you first.'

Mia gave a sideways glance of triumph that Madison clocked instantly. 'Actually, both just come together.'

Justin instantly started to make whining noises, throwing down his dinosaur toys and dragging his feet. Normal toddler tantrums actually didn't bother Madison that much. She hurried them both in the shower and had them dried and in pyjamas within ten minutes.

'Say goodnight to Dr Fletch and say thank you for the dinosaurs,' she prompted.

'I want to stay up,' said Mia.

Justin didn't make the same objections. He was tired. He wandered through to the main room and gave Fletch an interested look. 'Thanks for the rex,' he said. 'Night-night.' Then he turned, went to his own room, and climbed into his bed. 'Kiss, Mummy.'

Madison kissed her son, stroked his hair and murmured in his ear. 'Love you, darling.'

His eyes closed instantly, but Madison knew he wouldn't sleep right through. He hadn't in weeks.

Mia was more of a challenge. By the time Madison came back through she was sitting on the sofa next to Fletch with her favourite book in hand. Fletch was obediently reading to her, with a grin on his face.

'I do as I'm told,' he murmured as Madison sat down next to them both.

Her daughter was a feisty little character, and, while she would never let her be rude or overbearing, she didn't ever want to dampen her enthusiasm or curiosity. Somehow, she didn't think Mia would ever be anyone's fool.

Mia shot her mother a look and Madison nearly laughed out loud. Mia had got her own way. She made Fletch read her three different stories before Madison finally herded her off to bed.

When she came back through, she hesitated in the doorway. Fletch was sitting comfortably on the sofa, wine glass in hand, watching the TV.

It caught her right in the gut.

This was the first time she'd had another guy back to her place—like this—since Jason had died.

Shouldn't she be crying right now? Regretting she'd asked him over? Because although it felt a little odd, it didn't feel wrong. Did that mean that she was ready to try something new?

There wasn't anyone to have this conversation with, or pose these questions to, so Madison went with her instincts.

She crossed back into the room, picked up her glass of wine and sat back down next to him. 'What do you think?'

Fletch looked thoughtful. 'I'm still in a process of elimination. I think we look at inflammatory responses next with a more specific blood test, or even a few simple scans. His joints bother him, that's clear. And the irritation—could that actually be an underlying mild inflammation in the cerebral tissues?'

Madison started and he reached over and touched her arm. 'Don't be alarmed. I have to think of everything.'

She nodded but couldn't help but be scared. The normal cause of that kind of thing was meningitis. 'He's had all his jabs,' she murmured. 'But that doesn't rule out viral meningitis.'

Fletch shook his head. 'His symptoms would be more acute if he had a viral strain of meningitis.'

'I guess so.' His hand was still on her arm and she looked down at it. The feel of his fingers on her skin was warm and comforting. It was also starting a series of tingles up the length of her arm.

He hadn't mentioned her sloppy, comfortable clothes. She wasn't sure he'd even noticed. They didn't seem to bother him, and that made her glad, because the girl in the uniform at work, the girl in the dress at the orchid garden, was—nine times out of ten— the girl in yoga pants at home.

She lifted her head and his pale green eyes met hers. 'The kids have gone to bed,' he whispered. 'Do you want me to go?'

Her reaction was instant and she shook her head. She really, really didn't want him to go.

But her nerves were honestly shredded.

Before she had a chance to think, Fletch leaned forward until his lips were inches from hers and she could feel his warm breath. 'How about we relax and watch a movie? If Justin wakes up in the next few hours I'll be able to see what he's like.'

He hadn't asked if he could kiss her. But the closeness was invitation enough for Madison. Kissing him now would release the pent-up frustration in her stomach and mind, about wondering whether it might ever happen tonight or not.

She brushed her lips against his and he didn't hesitate to reciprocate. His hands were in her hair a few seconds later, then his lips were on her throat as her fingers ran along the stubble on his jaw. She could taste him, she could smell him. It was like dipping her toe in the waters of intimacy again, and every cell in her body was switched on. She wanted to laugh out loud that she still worked. She'd wanted to joke in the past that those parts of her had probably died, but it would have been so inappropriate to say those words out loud. So she'd only thought them, in her own head, in her own space, as part of her grieving process.

Her own fingers climbed up into his dark hair, and she resisted the urge to pull on it, instead taking a breath and separating her lips from his.

He rested his forehead against hers. He was smiling. She could see his lips and his teeth, and he was breathing hard.

She didn't need to say the rest. That she wasn't ready to go any further. That this wasn't the time and the place. Because Fletch just got that naturally.

He slung his arm around her shoulders, and relaxed as she snuggled in beside him, trying to still her thudding heart. She picked up the remote and scanned the movies available.

They both started laughing as *Top Gun* and its sequel appeared. 'We can't scroll on by,' said Fletch. 'Original, or new?'

'Let's go with something new,' she said. The words felt natural, and she closed her eyes for a second at the double meaning.

'Sure,' he said easily and selected the movie. Madison relaxed back and put her hand on his chest, letting the next few hours be full of supersonic speed, eye-watering manoeuvres and some iconic theme tunes.

CHAPTER EIGHT

FLETCH WAS STRANGELY comfortable in his skin. And that made him uncomfortable.

What made this worse was that he felt as if he was always pretty comfortable at the start of a relationship—when things were new, when the attraction sparked, and when his head was permanently full of the newest woman.

But that made his insides curl. Because, deep down, the feelings he had now didn't parallel how he'd felt around a woman before. This seemed...different.

And if you asked him to take a notebook and write down all the differences? He doubted he could.

That was what was so odd about everything. Last night, of course, he'd wanted to push things on. But he'd known Madison wanted to control the pace and he was fine with that.

And he wasn't an idiot. He didn't want either of Madison's children seeing something untoward. Children talked. And he wasn't sure if Madison had told them she might date other people—or how that would go down with her extended family.

Fletch had been in complicated relationships before, and he'd always been happy to just go with the flow. This time? He was nervous in a way he hadn't been before.

So much confusion around all this.

And then there was Justin. It had been interesting watching him undisturbed in his natural habitat. It gave Fletch the chance to see all the little idiosyncrasies and how they affected the child.

He got what Madison was saying. He also understood why she was likely feeling paranoid about everything. It was such a collection of seemingly unconnected symptoms. Some paediatricians might think along neurodivergent lines, but Fletch wasn't convinced.

He sighed and pushed back from his chair, trying to concentrate on work. He had twenty patients to see as outpatients this afternoon and another seven to review on the ward.

As he walked out of his office and along the corridor, he heard Madison speaking to one of the junior doctors. Their voices were hushed.

'Anything I can help with?' he asked.

Madison was in her dark blue uniform, her hair pulled high in a ponytail. 'I think I'm just stepping on a few toes,' she said, clearly trying to keep her voice light.

'Do you have concerns about a patient?' asked Fletch reasonably.

She nodded. 'I've got a suspicion about a new admission.'

Fletch held out his hands for the notes and the other doctor started talking. 'Two years old with respiratory symptoms, some swelling and a cough.'

Madison added, 'The cough is like a bark, and there's definite stridor.' She leaned over him looking at the notes. 'Do we know the vaccination history of the child, and where they flew in from?'

Fletch met her gaze and knew what her suspicions were. 'Unusual,' he said to her.

'What?' asked the junior doctor.

'Let's go and see,' said Fletch. 'Come with us, Madison, if you don't mind.'

She gave a nod and followed them into the patient's single room. She gestured to the junior doctor to follow her lead, washing her hands and donning a plastic apron and face mask. Fletch was repeating the motions at another sink in the room.

He introduced himself to the parent, and started to examine the little girl. 'When did she start to become unwell?' he asked.

'A few days ago. It seemed like a cold, and she had a sore throat, but things have just got more severe since then.'

'Has she had her routine childhood immunisations?'

There was a few moments' silence and the man shook his head. 'No, we've moved about a lot and haven't managed to get them completed. We've been so busy.'

'Can you give me an idea of what countries you've been in?'

'India, Malaysia, Vietnam, Haiti, and Africa.'

Fletch gave a nod. 'I'm going to take a look at Rimi's throat.' He encouraged the child to open her throat and shone a pen torch inside. He caught a glimpse of something and gave Madison a knowing look. 'Dr Yan, can you see the unusual colouring?'

Dr Yan nodded. 'The membranes look grey.'

Fletch nodded and then started pressing his finger very gently into Rimi's throat. 'You mentioned swelling, but this is unusual and is characteristic of a particular condition. This kind of swelling of the throat is called a bull neck.'

He turned to the parent. 'I'm going to do some blood work and some swabs, but most importantly Rimi's symptoms make me think she might have diphtheria. We're going to get her started on antibiotics right away. She'll need some inhalers and oxygen too.'

He turned to Sister Rui Lee, who had appeared at his side as if by some unknown antenna. 'I'll get a cardiac monitor and assign someone to monitor her closely,' she said, bustling away.

'Why does she need a cardiac monitor?' asked the parent. He was right next to Madison and she turned and spoke softly to him. 'Diphtheria can cause myocarditis— inflammation of the heart muscle— which can cause irregular heartbeats. That's why they'll put her on a cardiac monitor for now.'

Fletch gave her a nod, and also pointed to Rimi's throat. 'We have to keep a careful eye on the swelling of the throat. If it starts to obstruct Rimi's breathing, we'll have to talk again.'

He stayed there a few minutes longer, applying cream to allow the insertion of the cannula for the IV antibiotics, and talking through things with the parents, taking notes of all possible carriers and contacts.

As he walked back down the corridor, still making notes on the tablet, he gave a loud sigh. Madison followed him into the office and closed the door. 'I can't believe they didn't get their kid vaccinated. Don't they know diphtheria can kill?'

'Clearly not,' said Fletch, shaking his head. 'And I will have that conversation with them later. In the meantime I have to hope this isn't going to end up in a tracheostomy for this little girl—that would lead to permanent scarring.'

Madison's face was pale. He could tell she was thinking about her own kids. 'They moved about a bit and were just too busy to get the jabs done.' She blinked back tears as she murmured back the parent's words. 'I hope this doesn't have consequences they'll regret for the rest of their lives.'

Fletch took a deep breath. 'Vaccine is a choice, but it's difficult to understand why parents—if they do want to get their child vaccinated—just don't prioritise it, and take the fifteen minutes it takes to attend an appointment with their child. Most people think the diseases we vaccinate against are virtually non-existent now. They don't realise they can be fatal until something like this happens.' He leaned over and put his head in his hands. 'Rimi has severe throat swelling. I'm going to have to stay here tonight, in case her throat obstructs.'

'Are you on call?'

He nodded. 'And usually I go home, and just come in if required. But not tonight.' He shook his head. 'I can't take that risk. If Rimi deteriorates I want to be here.' He took a breath. 'I also want to be here to support Dr Yan. Can you imagine being the junior doctor on duty with a child like that on the ward overnight?' He shook his head. 'It will be a learning experience, but I'm going to make sure I'm right here on his shoulder if he needs me.'

'And I'm sure he'll appreciate it.'

Fletch looked around her and glanced at the closed door, before leaning forward and taking her hand. 'I was going to ask you if we could take the kids to the play park for an hour—just so I could watch them again.'

'Watch them, or watch me?' she asked, with a half-smile. She was only teasing, and he knew it. But she was closer to the mark than she thought.

'Definitely both, but I'm sorry. Not this evening.'

'Where will you sleep?' she asked him.

He was aware that although some physios in some departments—like ICU—would be on call overnight, Madison didn't have that kind of role.

'There's a room for the junior doctor just outside the ward area, and there's a room for the on-call consultant on the next floor. Believe me, I've slept in worse.'

'I'm just glad you're happy to do it.' Madison smiled. 'Makes me know I've picked the right doctor for my kid.'

His heart gave a little jump. Yes, this was a compliment. And that was the way it was meant. But it was also a reminder to him about treating the child of a friend. And he didn't think of Madison as a friend. He thought of her as, potentially, so much more.

She moved over and gave him a quick hug. 'I have to get back to work. Text me later if you want.'

'Hold on.' He scribbled something on a prescription pad. 'I talked Rimi's parents through the fact they'll need to take a course of antibiotics. Can you ask them to go and get these at the hospital pharmacy, and start them straight away?'

'Absolutely.' She disappeared out of the office and left Fletch considering what next. He reviewed Rimi for the next few hours. But also spent some time considering Justin. He ordered a few tests on the blood sample already taken. He'd take more bloods if he really had to.

He also ordered a simple ultrasound of Justin's joints. It wasn't invasive, only required gel, and a probe, and chances were Madison would actually be able to read the results herself straight away. If anything, it might give her reassurance.

But cases like these could be difficult. There was always the chance of ruling out just about every possible considered diagnosis, and still being no further forward. Frustrating for doctor, parent and sometimes the patient. For a second he thought about what that might do to his relationship with Maddie, before instantly pushing it away.

He was too thorough, too ethical to even consider that thought. So, he continued to consider other options, sporadically going out and discussing Rimi with Dr Yan, checking her swelling, monitoring her heart rate and administration of intravenous antibiotics and overseeing some steroids too, anything to try and delay the consequences of the disease.

He knew he was being ultra-cautious, and also that he had to have some faith in his junior doctor, so he made his way up to the sleeping quarters. It was comfortable enough, with a single bed, a desk, a chair, a TV and a separate shower room and bathroom. But it was what was sitting in the middle of the bed that stopped him. Normally, the hospital housekeeping staff would make the bed and leave fresh scrubs and towels. This time there was also a little basket with a pile of goodies.

He moved forward, his eyes scanning the basket. Crisps, chocolate, biscuits, a peach, some jellies and a little note.

Something to see you through the night. M

Something washed over him as he sat on the edge of the bed. It was like a tidal wave of warmth, and part of him told him that he shouldn't be feeling this.

He'd only been with her a few times. What if he changed his mind later? What if this was all just the normal rush of first meeting someone—when you wanted to spend every second with them?

But everything about this made him scared. That was what was different here.

Because he liked her. He really liked her. And liking her meant he was moving away from who he was, and who he'd ever been. Fletch, the serial dater. Fletch, 'not the next stage'. Fletch, the man who'd managed to stay on good terms with all exes, because they knew exactly who he was.

But what would happen if he wasn't that person any more?

Madison was trying to find her new normal. As Jason's parents collected the kids for their overnight stay, she waved them off, and wondered if Mia or Justin would mention Fletch.

She had told them that she'd asked the new doctor to try and help her get to the bottom of why her son was so irritable and tired these days. She'd also been truthful and said he'd spent some time with the kids, trying to assess Justin. It wasn't a lie at all. It just wasn't the complete truth. And that didn't sit well with Madison. Because she loved Jason's parents dearly. They were important people who she would always want to feature in her life.

Fletch had sent her a message telling her to dress up and wear her favourite high heels.

She was excited. She liked being a grown-up again.

This time she was wearing a green dress, and a spectacular pair of multicoloured heels. She'd dried her hair with some curls and was ready to go as soon as Fletch appeared at the door.

He was more formally dressed than last time, wearing a pair of trousers and shoes and a short-sleeved shirt and jacket. She tipped her head. 'You scrub up well,' she said, unable to stop smiling.

Fletch let out a low wolf whistle. 'Loving the shoes,' he said admiringly.

Madison tilted them from side to side. 'As my gran in Scotland would say, they're a pair of wee crackers!'

Fletch laughed at her thick Scottish accent and held out his elbow to her. 'Are we ready to go?'

She nodded and enjoyed their walk along the streets and on to the MRT, even though she had no idea where they were going.

'Is this going to be the thing for us?' she asked.

'What?'

'That you whisk me onto the MRT and I never know where we're heading.'

He gave her a playful look. 'Would you like a hint?'

She held up her fingers. 'Just a tiny one.'

He leaned over, his nose brushing against her cheek, sending shivers down her spine as he whispered in her ear. 'We're going to do the corniest thing possible in Singapore.'

She sat back and looked at him with a mix of interest and suspicion. 'Should I be scared?'

He laughed. 'Oh, no, definitely not scared. You might even like it.'

She settled back and slid her hand into his, liking the way it felt to be connected to someone. They chatted easily as the smooth train continued and after a short time Fletch gave her a look and leaned forward. 'This is us.'

Esplanade station had seven exits, and as Fletch steered her towards exit E her heart started to miss a few beats. 'Are you serious?' she asked.

Fletch kept his face entirely straight as they walked a few yards from the exit and stood underneath the famous bright white towering façade, with red roof. 'Raffles?' She grinned.

It was one of the most famous hotels in the world. She put her hand on her hip. 'You did say we were doing the corniest thing possible.' She licked her lips and put her hands around his neck. 'And I can't wait.'

Fletch was steadily losing every nerve he'd ever had. He'd always thought of himself as a cool guy. His friends joked about it— as did his exes. He was the guy that never panicked, never flapped, always kept a cool head, and even temper. But around Madison, he felt anything but cool. He felt like a nervous wreck who was turning temporarily into a simmering volcano that could erupt at any second. It was like being an excitable teenager again—and nobody wanted that, least of all him.

'Ready to get a drink?' he asked, knowing there was a glint in his eye.

Madison was beaming. He loved when she looked like this. Ready to take on the world.

Right now, Madison didn't look like a woman who'd been widowed. She didn't look like the mum to two small kids, one of whom kept her awake most nights. Right now, Madison Koh looked as if she were ready to take on and conquer the world—albeit in a very sexy way.

She sashayed as she walked up the steps to the lobby of Raffles hotel, nodding at the doorman and taking a deep breath as they walked in. The lobby was spectacular, bright white, with floor-to-ceiling Victorian pillars and black wrought-iron railings on the floor above. The sense of space was immense. In the middle was the biggest chandelier Fletch had ever seen and the beautiful flower displays around them gave the place a splash of colour.

'Would you care to visit the Long Bar?' he asked.

'I absolutely would.' She grinned back as her high heels resounded off the tiled floor.

They walked through to the iconic Long Bar. The bar was highly polished with a set of high chairs along its length. A variety of tables and chairs filled the rest of the space, and a barman gestured to them both to have a seat.

Madison headed for the traditional leather bar chair, hitching her dress a little to climb up. Fletch joined her and the barman set down coasters and a bowl of peanuts in front of them. 'What will it be, sir? Madam?'

They glanced at each other and echoed the words that Fletch was quite sure the barman never wanted to hear again in his life.

'Singapore Slings.' Both of them started to laugh, and, to his credit, the barman was completely nonplussed and smiled graciously. They both watched, transfixed as he made the gin-based cocktail for them both, setting down the chilled glasses with the pink mixture inside.

They clinked their drinks together and took a sip. Delicious.

'How often have you done this?' Fletch asked her.

'Twice,' she said, then paused. 'No, maybe three times. I think I came here as part of a very expensive hen dinner once. But it may be blanked from my mind.'

Her hen do? Fletch was almost scared to ask. 'You can't leave it like that. You have to tell me.'

She bent her head low. 'It was the friend of a friend. And she was very late. We'd been sitting at dinner for more than an hour before she showed, and, in that time, we'd had a few cocktails. By the time she arrived, she was hysterical, screaming the wedding was off, as she'd seen her groom with someone else.'

'What? No way?'

Madison gave a quiet laugh. 'Oh, it gets worse. The bride normally wore glasses, but she'd got contacts for her wedding and wasn't really used to them yet, or particularly good at getting them in or out.'

Fletch put his head in his hands. 'No, she didn't.'

Madison nodded. 'Oh, she did. She hadn't put her contacts in properly. In fact, it ended up as a hospital visit since she'd managed to lose one in her eye somehow. But she'd phoned her father to call the wedding off. Phoned the groom's mother to shout at her. And, of course, she'd mistaken some other guy for her own fiancé. It was a bit of a mess.' She nodded slowly. 'But more importantly, we never got dinner because of all the fiasco, which meant the cocktails went straight to my head, I'm not sure if I had a Singapore Sling or not, and I ended up home, in my bed.'

He tapped the bar. 'But you didn't tell the best bit. Did the wedding go ahead?'

She raised her eyebrows. 'What's your guess?'

He held up his hands, then leaned his chin on one. 'I have no idea. But I won't be able to sleep tonight if you don't tell me.'

He loved this. He loved this chat about nonsense. The chance to see the fun side of Madison and leave all the other stuff to one side. Their jobs. Their past lives. And just to be two people, on a date, flirting, and having fun.

The bartender appeared again and Fletch realised their glasses were empty. 'Same again?'

Madison shook her head. 'I'll have a Negroni this time, please.'

'And I'll have a Sazerac, please.'

The bartender disappeared with a nod.

It was early evening and the place was starting to fill up. All the other clientele were discreet, sitting quietly at their tables or the bar and chatting. 'Wonder what it will be like in here later,' mused Madison. 'It's such a classy place.'

'Well, it sounds like you and your friends managed to get all hen parties barred from coming to Raffles a few years ago.'

'At least ten,' she said as she thought. 'And to be honest, I remember being surprised that they'd taken the booking in the first place. I'm sure her mother or sister must have lied and said it was a family dinner.'

As the bartender set down their fresh coasters, glasses and a small dish of olives, Fletch touched her hand.

'I meant it. You need to tell me the end of that story.'

'Ah,' said Madison carefully, tapping her fingers on the bar. 'About that...' She let her voice tail off.

'Yes?' he asked.

'Well, it got even more complicated. Her father had immediately cancelled the venue. His mother had gone around to the bride's house in a rage. A huge fight ensued, and the poor groom came home completely bewildered by everything that was going on. By this point, the bride had realised it was all her mistake and was hysterical. The groom's mother had flounced off and said she'd had enough of everything. And the bride's mother was too busy ranting about how all this had caused her embarrassment and made her lose face with her friends.'

Fletch held up one hand. 'Okay, stop. This is turning into a story that my auntie Mary tells me when I ask one question, and I'm still waiting to get it answered ten minutes later.'

Madison gave him her best conspiratorial look. 'I swear, even if I let you have a thousand guesses you would never get what happened next!'

Fletch, never one to resist a challenge, held up one hand and started counting off. 'They lived happily ever after. They never spoke to each other again. One, or the other, just used the wedding as a giant party, so things didn't go to waste.'

Madison shook her head smugly.

'Okay, let me go for thriller-writer mode, then—one went on the honeymoon and ended up dead?'

Madison raised her eyebrows.

'I've got it,' said Fletch triumphantly. 'One caught an extremely rare, non-identifiable disease—that originated in the ice age and came from the melting polar ice caps—and is currently in a top-secret facility somewhere.'

She narrowed her gaze and gave a half-smile. 'I'm beginning to wonder if I should have second thoughts about you. I really wonder what goes on in that head of yours.'

'Only second thoughts?' he teased. 'I thought we'd be at least third or fourth by this stage.'

She kept her elbows leaning on the bar and gave him a hard stare.

'Okay,' he relented. 'I give up. What is it?'

Madison crossed her legs again, and couldn't help but notice his gaze landing on her bare skin. She stayed quiet for a second until his eyes rose again to meet hers.

'Busted,' he murmured good-naturedly.

'You want to know?' she asked again.

He nodded.

'Then you picked the wrong theme. Thriller wasn't what you were looking for—or sci-fi. You should have stuck with romance. It turned out the bride's father met the groom's mother in amongst the fights and cancellations. Love blossomed, and they married the next year.'

'No way.' He was frowning. He shot her a sideways glance. 'I take it the bride and groom weren't too happy?'

She raised her glass to him and finished her cocktail. 'It's very safe to say that they were not. But by that point—' she grinned '—nobody cared!'

He laughed and shook his head, taking another glance around at their opulent surroundings. 'You sure know how to spin a story.'

'But isn't it fun?' She held up one hand, 'And just think of the history of this building. Think of the amount of stories that are actually held in this place.'

She couldn't hide her enthusiasm or the wonder she was feeling right now. It had been so long since she'd let her hair down like this, had a few drinks with a handsome man, forgot about life and its responsibilities for a few hours.

'I should bring you out more often,' said Fletch, his head resting on his hand and his eyes full of admiration, and something else.

Madison stretched out her arms. 'I'm a very expensive date. Then, a very troublesome one. You'll get bored of me quickly.'

'I don't think so.' He smiled as he shook his head. 'What do you want to do next? Some dinner again?'

'How about something different?'

'What?'

'Marina Bay. The light show. It's been a few years since I've seen it.'

Fletch stood up instantly and checked his watch. 'It's on at eight and nine. Think we'll make the nine o'clock show?'

She looked down at her multicoloured heels. 'I refuse to take these off to run. The MRT will get us there in plenty of time. The Bayfront station is only a short walk from the viewing deck.'

'Let's go, then.'

They left the beauty of Raffles hotel, and descended back onto the smooth-running MRT, alighting at Bayfront station and taking the walk to the viewing deck for the water, light and music show.

The deck was already crowded with a mixture of tourists and locals. The show was performed twice a night usually, with an extra ten o'clock show on a Friday and Saturday night.

A trombone was playing loudly at a nearby bar restaurant as they watched everyone adjust their positions for the show. As soon as the background music for the light and water show started, the trombone halted, allowing everyone to be entranced by the display.

It was dazzling. It started softly. The colours muted, the water shooting up in bright jets of light in perfect time. But things started to build. The tempo increased, the colours darkened, deep purples and blue, with whirling pinks that shot out brilliantly. Greens and oranges lit the sky as the fountain spurts grew larger. Yellow circular displays appeared like giant suns. What had started in quite a small, concentrated space filled the whole area in front of them, with water spurting from parts that had previously been dry, much to the delight of some of the crowd who were hit by tiny spots of backlash water.

Things grew to a crescendo, with a rainbow of coordinated colours appearing at once, alongside the vibrant music and perfectly directed water fountains.

Madison rested back against Fletch. His arms wrapped around her waist and settled across her stomach. His head positioned behind her head and shoulders. It was the most relaxed she'd felt in the last three years. She felt…safe.

Before she had time to focus on those thoughts, Fletch's lips were trailing along the side of her face. She leaned back into him more, giving him access to the skin at her neck as she tipped her head back. It was easy to flip around, wrap her hands around his neck and meet him head-on.

The lights and water were still erupting around them as if the whole display had been put on entirely for them. At least, that was how it felt.

And that fed into the wave of sensations she was feeling right now. The wall that she had between her and Fletch was gradually eroding. She was doing her best to keep it in place, but it didn't help when he touched her like this. When his lips made her lose focus and struggle to breathe.

A tiny part of her brain moved into panic mode. In a few years' time would Fletch refer to her as his Singapore fling? Would he leave when his contract ended without a second glance, and with Madison on his phone as one of his many friends? Because she didn't want to be his friend.

She wanted more than that. And that re-alisation was causing her momentary panic.

She pulled back, and spun around so he couldn't see her shocked face. She was already breathless, so her racing heart didn't really matter.

He was a serial dater. She was a mother with twins. Her kids had to be her priority. She wondered how other women did this. Not just those who were widowed, but those who had divorced, had a failed relationship behind them, or had chosen to have children on their own. How did they navigate the dating world? And how would she feel if the shoe were on the other foot? If Fletch were widowed with twins, and she had happily dated one guy after another, with no permanency and no bad feelings.

Putting the shoe on the other foot was illuminating in a way she didn't particularly like.

Would she consider taking on someone else's children and loving them just as much as if they were her own? She wasn't naïve. Of course, she had friends both male and female who'd found themselves in this position. But she'd never actually sat down and asked them the questions that now circled around her brain—because part of her knew she would be heartbroken if she didn't like the answers.

She tried to concentrate. To think about

her friends who'd met a partner who already had children. Madison's trouble was, the people she could think about were all shining examples of things working well. Of embracing their new life, and, after a few hiccups, becoming a real integrated family.

Was it wrong that she wished for that too?

She thought back to her chats as a teenager. Being convinced that there would only ever be one great love in her life. Then meeting Jason, and thinking she was set for life.

She still had friends who were single. Who had never met their Ms or Mr Right. Was it too much to wish for two such people in her life?

'Hey,' came the low voice in her ear. 'Where are you? I think I've lost you.'

She jerked just as a cool breeze swept past them. 'Sorry,' she said automatically. 'Thinking about work.'

There was a flash of puzzlement on his face, and she wanted to cringe at her unlikely untruth. The rest of the people around them had started to leave, the light show finished.

'Food?' he asked again, and he seemed hopeful. But her stomach was unsettled. She wasn't sure she could cope with food.

'Actually, I'm feeling kind of tired. Can you take me home?'

She saw the fleeting disappointment on his face and let it sink in. In an imaginary world he'd take her back to Raffles and check into a thousand-pounds-a-night suite. They'd spend all night in bed and wake up in luxury with no worries at all.

But Madison didn't live in that world. She lived in this one.

Fletch was gracious and put his arm around her shoulder, walking back to the MRT and stopping to buy them coffee on the way. He didn't seem worried that the rest of world was only just starting their Saturday nights, while theirs was being cut short.

It had started so magically and full of fun and Madison couldn't explain what had come over her. All of a sudden she was hit with so many doubts.

And she knew exactly why. Whether Fletch knew it or not, this relationship was taking a turn for her. She'd been happy to keep things private and just go along for the ride to begin with to test her dating wings again.

It had been nice to have adult conversations and feel special again. But she couldn't trust herself. If she let herself truly buy into this, she could end up with a whole host of hurt. Even though she liked to act invincible and sassy, her outer shell wasn't as hard as she'd like it to be. And her insides? They were just a mixed-up pool of melted chocolate and giant brownies.

They rode in silence, sipping coffee. He still had his arm around her shoulder, and she was leaning into him as if she'd been born to do it.

'Madison?' The heavily accented voice brought her sharply to her senses. Fletch jerked right alongside her and removed his arm from her shoulder.

Koreen Choi appeared in front of Madison. As usual, the childhood friend of Jason was stylishly dressed in bright colours. With her sharp pixie cut and small figure she could have graced the cover of any of the high-fashion magazines. She couldn't hide the curious glance towards Fletch, before leaning forward and kissing Madison on one cheek, and then the other.

'How are you? How are my babies?'

Madison tried to pretend that this was the most normal thing in the world, and she wasn't entirely in shock. Of course, there was always a chance that she was going to come across a friend of hers and Jason's, or a colleague from work anywhere in Singapore. It didn't matter that it was a place of more than five million people.

'Justin and Mia are good. They spent some time with my mum and dad in Scotland just over a month ago, and I'm just trying to get them back into a routine.' She gave Koreen a big smile. 'You should give me a call and come and visit us some time. They'd be happy to see you.'

Madison was totally aware that every part of her body was tense, while she gave the pretence this was a normal everyday conversation. She was aware when Koreen's eyes drifted back to Fletch. She couldn't avoid this. She wouldn't be rude to someone who had always been friendly and supportive. 'Koreen, this is Fletch. He's a new paediatrician working with us at St David's.'

There was a gleam of curiosity in Koreen's eyes, but she held out her hand instantly towards Fletch. 'It's so nice to meet you. I'm an old-time friend of Madison and the family. Are you enjoying St David's?'

Fletch nodded amiably, but Madison knew that he, too, was tense. 'I am. I've worked in Singapore before and was delighted to come back.'

'Back for good?'

He hesitated. 'I have a two-year contract right now. I'll wait and see.'

Madison's insides coiled in a way they had

absolutely no right to. Her brain was telling her she knew this. Her brain was talking in a very firm voice saying that she was nowhere near the point she could have that conversation with Fletch about staying for longer. She had no right.

But her body was listening. Her body was protesting. Her scary cynical gene was yelling at her, saying he never cracked a joke about maybe being 'back for good'.

Madison was always amazed by just how many sensations and thoughts could spring through the mind in the literal blink of an eye.

Sometimes she wished her brain would fixate on bouncing sheep, unicorns, rainbows—even the latest kids' TV show. But no, her brain wanted to torture her on a daily basis with doubts and uncertainties.

'Well, good luck,' Koreen said cheerily before focusing back on Madison with eyes that already sized up exactly what was going on. 'Here's my stop. I'll give you a call, gorgeous, and pop up and see my favourites.'

She gave Madison a wink and made her way back down the carriage to the door. Stepping out as they arrived at the station, her bright pink coat disappearing into the crowd.

Madison swallowed. Her skin was cold and her heart was racing. The dress and shoes now seemed like overkill.

'Who was that?' asked Fletch quietly.

'A friend of Jason's family.'

'Are you worried about what she might say?'

It was a perfectly reasonable question, and she knew that. But in one sense it seemed like a criticism, and in another it made her want to defend herself.

In the end, she sagged back against the chair. 'I haven't told anyone about us.'

'I know.'

She turned to face him, feeling a bit surprised.

'You said at the beginning you didn't want people at work to know. I respect that.'

'But you haven't told anyone else?' She was thinking of his myriad exes that he texted all the time. Did no one know she actually existed?

'No. Do you think Koreen will say something to Jason's family?'

There they were. The words that made her heart feel as if a giant spear had just pierced it. 'I don't know. I don't think so. She's not like that. Not malicious, I mean.' Madison's hand went automatically to her hair, twisting it around one finger. 'I just haven't mentioned anything to Jason's parents, or his sister. I mean, I'm sure they'll expect me to date again at some point. I just don't know if they'll expect that point to be now.'

Fletch's eyes were fixed on her in a steady stare. 'I think, no matter what the timescale, it might be hard to have that conversation.'

There he was. Being all reasonable again.

'I know that.' She sighed. 'I just want them to be okay about it. I don't want them to hate me. Or to think I've forgotten about Jason.'

He didn't try and placate her with words. He just put his hand over hers. 'You won't know until you have that conversation. And you shouldn't have that conversation until you're ready.'

She closed her eyes for a second. 'But there's the kids as well. What if they mention you've been to the apartment?'

Fletch shrugged. 'That's up to you. You either say I'm Justin's doctor, or that I'm your friend.' He paused for a second. 'Or, that we're dating. Your call.'

She hated that. She hated that he made it all seem so uncomplicated.

'Kids don't keep secrets. We know that. They don't really understand the concept, and in lots of ways that's a good thing. Just do what you think is best.'

'What is best?' she asked.

Fletch looked surprised. But not as much as she was. She hadn't expected to say those words out loud. Maybe this was because they'd kept their relationship secret. She hadn't had anyone to talk to about it. Now the only person it made sense to talk to was him.

There was a long pause. 'I can't tell you that. Maybe it's time for us to reconsider.'

She could swear a chill breeze blew over her skin. 'What do you mean?'

Was that her voice? There was an edge of panic in it. Definitely not cool. She was so out of practice with all this stuff.

He leaned a little closer. 'I mean, is it time to tell people? Is it time to let colleagues at work know that we are dating?'

Relief flooded through her. She'd thought he was going to suggest they call things quits.

She wrinkled her nose. 'Do we tell people at work before I tell Jason's family—or my own?'

'Your own family is in Scotland. You can tell them whenever you like. Does Jason's family have friends that work in the hospital—would they hear if we started letting people know we were dating?' He held up his hands. 'If they won't, then telling our colleagues might give you some idea as to how Jason's old workmates will act. If you think it could get back, you might want to talk to his family and just mention that you're considering dating again.'

'What if I break their hearts?'

He shook his head and closed both hands over hers. 'Madison, their hearts were broken three years ago when their son died. Nothing changes that.' His voice was low and calm. 'I don't know these people at all. But I hope that they love you and the kids as much as you love them—and it sounds like it. Maybe they'll feel a bit sensitive to it. Maybe, they'll think that it's time. To be honest, I have no idea. But the most important thing is that you do this when you're ready. These people are family for you and the kids. I can't give you an opinion on this.'

She breathed slowly, trying to still her thoughts. The night had started so well, dressing up for fun cocktails. Watching the beautiful fountains and lights. But something had halted her enjoyment, and she was wise enough to know this was all about her, and not about Fletch.

She was racked by self-doubts. And she hated herself for it.

The train drew into their station and they climbed out. She'd left him at her doorway before. And she was going to do it again.

But Fletch seemed to know. He hesitated at the elevator in her apartment and kissed her on the cheek. 'Need some time to think?'

She nodded, blinking back tears she really, really didn't want him to see.

'Thank you,' she whispered, then pressed the button quickly before she could see him walk away.

Because somehow, she knew, that vision would imprint on her brain.

CHAPTER NINE

FLETCH WAS DOING his best to play it cool.

This was it. This was his time to decide if it was make or break.

He'd been at this point at several times in his life. And it had always been break.

Break was the lesser of two evils. Or at least, that was how he'd always felt before.

Because his heart had never really been involved before. And this time it was right in the middle of things. No one woman had ever had the effect that Madison had on him.

And because of that, this time was the first time he hadn't wanted to break. This time he wanted to make it.

And it was driving him crazy, because he wasn't sure that Madison felt the same.

He got that. She had more at stake. She could risk family fallouts, losing support systems she'd had in place for the last three years. Maybe that was just being dramatic, but it was still a potential risk.

What was his risk? Nothing. He had a time-limited contract.

But was his risk nothing, or did he just prefer to tell himself that? Otherwise, he might have to admit to having his heart broken for the first time. And that had never happened to Fletch before. He'd never been the one exposed before. He'd never invested himself so much in one person before.

Chills. That actually gave him chills. If he wanted to think long term with Madison, he would have to take on board the fact he would become a father figure to two ready-made kids. He liked Mia and Justin. But was he ready to go the full way? Was this the life he could see himself living?

He would have to step back from being Justin's doctor and he wasn't sure how Madison would feel about that.

It actually made every part of his brain switch on.

He had to face facts. It had been two weeks since Madison had brought Justin to see him. He'd ruled out a number of possible causes, but still nothing jumped out at him.

But if being Justin's doctor could stand in

the way of moving forward, maybe that was what he should concentrate on. Once he had a diagnosis for Justin, it would be reasonable to move his care over to another paediatrician.

And if he was concentrating on Justin, he wouldn't be contemplating the fact that Madison might decide this wasn't all worth it—that she wasn't quite ready to do this—and she wasn't as invested in Fletch as he was in her.

He couldn't believe how much that terrified him. That Madison might decide it wasn't worth it. *He* wasn't worth it. What if she thought Jason's family might dislike him? Or think it was too soon? What if all her friends and family just thought that Fletch wasn't the right person for her? There were so many outside influences. So many things outside his control. And at the centre of it all was Maddie.

He was staring out over Singapore from the darkness of his apartment. He'd realised the vibe had changed between them tonight, and thought she was backing off. It hadn't helped when they'd met her friend Koreen.

He could almost see her unravelling in front of him. If he was immature he'd be offended that she was worried about being seen with him. But he wasn't that pathetic. At least he hoped he wasn't.

He was trying to focus. He moved over to his laptop and flicked it open, starting to go through every possible condition, disease, virus, infection he could think of. When he'd finished with them, he went back through prenatal issues that could cause issues in children at a later date. When he'd finished all those, he looked at environmental issues, and unusually transmitted diseases. By four in the morning, he was exhausted, frustrated and very, very bad-tempered.

His fingers hovered over the keyboard again. Tomorrow, Madison might tell him she'd thought about it, and decided not to move forward. He'd have to gracefully accept that and step aside.

But he didn't want to. He wanted to stay and fight. But what was he fighting for? A chance just to keep dating her, or a chance to consider a future?

He liked her. He more than liked her. He thought about her all the time. He wanted to text her halfway through the night, then again when he was at work and had seen her only minutes before.

Sometimes, when he held her brown gaze,

he just wanted to reach out and hug her. Even when they were at work.

All of these emotions were new for him. All of them made him over the moon one second, and lower than the belly of a snake the next. Fletch was used to coasting. This roller coaster of emotions had taken him unawares and he was unprepared for the effects it was having on him. And it wasn't just Madison he thought about.

He liked spending time with the kids. Yes, Justin was still under the weather. But he was a good kid. Madison had made sure her children were polite, inquisitive and fun. Mia could run circles around him, and everyone else in a room. She was probably going to end up as a world leader at some point.

But could he realistically consider fitting into that family unit? What if the feelings he had right now for Madison slowly disappeared? Lots of people started relationships with enthusiasm that waned over a period of time. Some of his previous ones certainly had.

But, from the moment he'd met Madison, this whole thing had been different. It didn't matter he couldn't give a reason why. It was just something, deep down.

If he wanted to make this work, he had

to try and persuade Madison that he was a good option. But how exactly did he do that?

His eyes went back to the screen. Justin. He had to start with Justin, and his unknown ailment. Solve the first problem, and hope the rest would roll away.

Madison was walking on proverbial egg-shells. It had been a week, and nothing had been said between them about Saturday night. But Fletch had seen Justin twice more at hospital, and twice more when he'd suggested a reason for them all to spend time together.

She was trying to relax again. And she wondered about telling some of her colleagues she was dating Fletch. Would anyone actually care, or was she just overthinking things?

The range of tests on Justin was getting longer and longer. Thankfully, Fletch had arranged for the majority to be painless. The bloods he'd had taken at the beginning had been used for a number of other screens, but although Justin showed mild signs of inflammation and a small rise in white blood cells there wasn't anything else significant.

Now, they were focusing on background history. Everything he'd done or eaten in the last seven weeks. Part of this was hard, as Justin and Mia had been in Scotland with her parents for two weeks. But Madison's parents were very traditional people. They had relatively plain tastes when it came to food and hadn't taken the children anywhere unusual.

Madison already knew that her children would have frequented every tea shop in the village as her parents proudly showed them off to their friends, and would have spent hours in the local children's playground.

Her doorbell rang, and she answered, Justin already in her arms as he was cranky again. Fletch was standing in front of her holding up a bag.

'Ice cream?' he asked.

He hadn't told her he was coming over, and it was a shock to see his large frame and smiling face in the doorway. But what struck her most was how thankful she was to see him.

She swung open her door and waved him in, shouting over her shoulder. 'Mia, Fletch is here. He brought ice cream.'

The tiny figure dashed through, eyes shining. 'What kind?'

It was like an accusation rather than a question, and Fletch pretended to baulk. 'I have four, I'm sure you'll like one.'

'Don't count on it,' murmured Madison with a wry grin as she closed the door. She was wearing jeans and a T-shirt that was likely covered in stains and her hair was in a ponytail. She couldn't remember if she'd taken her make-up off or not, but was glad that Fletch hadn't given so much as a second glance to her dishevelled appearance.

'Want me to swap?' he asked, holding out his hands for Justin.

She hesitated. But Justin looked as if he was considering things, before finally holding his arms out towards Fletch.

Madison tried not to show her surprise. Justin was picky. He liked his crèche workers, Jason's family and a few select friends. But he'd obviously taken to Fletch.

Maybe it was his manner or his voice. Lots of kids on the wards reacted well to him. Fletch settled Justin on his hip and moved over to the kitchen table, gesturing to Mia to follow him. 'Why don't we sit down and let Mummy open the ice cream? Then we can decide what ones you like.'

Madison took the bag with a murmur of thanks and got four bowls and a variety of spoons from the cupboard. She set out the bowls, then put the ice-cream containers in the middle of the table, opening all the lids.

'Okay, we've got chocolate, vanilla, mint choc chip and strawberry.'

Madison was glad. Singapore had some of the fanciest ice creams and gelatos known to man, with flavours that adults would favour. She was relieved that Fletch had opted for the kids' kind of stuff.

Justin pointed to the vanilla. 'Is there sauce?'

Madison was about to say no. But Fletch nodded back over to the bag. 'Just some small ones.'

She double-checked and pulled out sachets of chocolate, caramel and raspberry.

'Sprinkles?' asked Mia hopefully.

'We have sprinkles,' said Madison and pulled them from the cupboard. She walked back over with the rest of the items. 'Right, is everyone happy? Can I sit back down?'

Two children nodded and she sat back down. The next half-hour was a mess of ice cream, sauce and sprinkles and the children had a ball. Fletch was so chilled around them, laughing and joking and asking questions about their favourite TV cartoon. He told them about one he'd watched as a kid, pulled it up on the Internet, where it was instantly dismissed by both of them.

Justin moved over from Fletch and back around to his mother, which meant he was getting tired again. As soon as he moved, Fletch picked up the bowls, wiped down the table and binned the containers. He nodded to Madison. 'Will I play a game with Mia?' and she gave a grateful smile as she took Justin off for a nap.

By the time she came back out, Mia and Fletch were on the floor in the living room doing a giant jigsaw together. Her heart melted a little. She knew he was making an effort and she appreciated it.

Before long they were sagged on the sofa together. Mia was sitting at the kids' table in the living room, colouring in. The whole afternoon had been impromptu, but she'd liked it. There hadn't been time to overthink things and get herself tied in knots. He didn't even blink when she flicked the TV and stuck on *Star Wars*.

It was so easy just to nestle into his arms and relax. 'I've been thinking,' she said after a while. 'Maybe it is time to start dropping some hints at the hospital.'

'You think?'

She licked her lips, wondering if he wanted to disagree with her. 'It just makes sense. I don't want to have to pretend about this when there are other people round. Or tell any lies. I think it would be okay if people knew we were dating.'

He gave a gentle nod. 'What about your family, and Jason's family? Do you think it's time to say anything to them?'

She tensed a little, knowing this was the hardest part. 'I was thinking of telling them this weekend that I was considering dating again, and that I'd been asked out.'

Her stomach was clenched, because it wasn't entirely the whole story. She wasn't going to give them Fletch's details and say who he was, but hopefully it would give them some time to get used to the idea before she would have to do introductions.

There was a slight pause, then Fletch shifted a little. 'How do you think that will go down?'

She sighed, her hand resting on his chest. 'I honestly don't know. I think if anything, they might be more worried about the kids being introduced to someone new, rather than me. And I'd be fine with that.'

'I get you wanting to tread carefully. But this is still your life to lead. You can't live it in hiding.'

'And I won't,' she said quickly. 'But I

haven't had to do this before, and I want to be sensitive.' Her eyes went to the corridor that led to Justin's room. 'I'm trying to think about it from their perspective.'

Fletch nodded. 'No parent should outlive their child. I get that. And I hate being on the other side of that as a physician. So, I understand. Let's just not be in the same position at a later date.'

There was no timescale attached, and her heart catapulted straight up. Fletch was here for two years—less than that now. But even saying a 'later date' meant he wasn't planning on bailing on her any time soon.

As his fingers traced small circles at the base of her neck she gave a pleasant shudder. This was nice. This was how she wanted things to be. She'd almost forgotten what the quiet moments were like. And now she'd had a few, she wanted them all the time.

She lifted her head slightly, and Fletch's lips were inches from hers. But instead of meetings her lips, he glanced in Mia's direction, and kissed Madison's forehead instead.

She almost laughed but instead she just settled back down to watch the movie. Was this what life could be like now?

She couldn't help but hope she was making the right decision.

* * *

Fletch was getting agitated. He'd had a number of cases over the years that had him stumped, but he hadn't expected to be stumped over a child he knew.

He'd been spending more and more time around Justin. He was developing a real understanding of this little boy's frustration. That horrible sensation of not feeling well, but not having the vocabulary to express it. The way he got impatient and tired easily. It was affecting his learning, and his ability to develop good social relationships with other children.

Fletch had noticed over the last few days, when he passed the crèche, that Justin was often isolated from the other children. Sometimes it was deliberate, and Justin was too tired to get involved in their games. But other times, the children were excluding Justin, maybe finding his behaviour difficult to understand and negotiate at the young age. As an adult, Fletch could see the staff trying their best to intervene, but it was difficult when Justin himself could prove reluctant.

Whatever was wrong was going to affect his long-term development, which made Fletch more determined to get to the bottom of it.

He even had a chart with everything he'd ruled out, and had discussed Justin casually with a number of other paediatricians he knew and trusted across the globe.

'I think you need to switch your brain off, and go with your gut,' said Darren, a friend from Ireland. 'Even if you can't find evidence of it, it can still be there.'

'Take the opposite approach from what you usually do,' urged Jules, a fellow paediatrician at a previous hospital he'd worked in. 'What if an adult presented to you with all these complaints and symptoms. Where would your brain go for them?'

Fletch took deep breaths and ran through the things he'd already considered. What did his gut tell him?

He started scribbling, doing a timeline. With children, things could be difficult. If children had an underlying developmental delay, it often didn't become apparent until this age, when children were more interactive and differences could be more noticeable.

He didn't compare Justin to Mia at all. Two entirely different children.

But two children who'd been brought up in the same environment, been exposed to the same things, and had similar experiences.

He was sitting in his office at work. Madison was by his side, flicking through her phone as she waited on a call back about taking one of her patients for a test.

The news of them dating had filtered out amongst the staff. Madison had told Rui, the ward sister, first. She'd been surprised, but hadn't made things awkward. A few people who'd been courteous to Fletch to begin with were now being a bit friendlier, asking him more questions. Were they making the effort because he was dating Madison? That was what it seemed like.

There had been a few hostile glares, and a few interested ones down in Radiology—the place that had been Justin's space. He was glad because he got the impression people were just getting on with their lives, instead of obsessing over him and Madison. And that was just perfect.

'The latest test results are back for Justin.' He scanned them and gave a sigh. 'I can't see anything of concern.'

The phone rang and he answered quickly. 'Dr Fletcher.'

The words had barely left his lips as he stood up, the chair falling behind him. He gripped Madison's shoulder. 'Of course, I'll come down. His mother is with me now. I'll bring her with me.'

Madison's face instantly paled. 'What is it?'

'Justin. That was the crèche. They said he's taken quite unwell. They'd phoned down to physio but couldn't get you.'

The two of them jogged down the corridor, lifting hands to other members of staff, so they didn't think there was an emergency on the ward.

It took only a few minutes to reach the crèche, where one of the workers was standing with Justin in her arms. She strode quickly over to meet them. 'He just became very lethargic, and he's quite breathless. He complained of pain in his chest, started crying and then became limp.'

Fletch assessed things quickly and lifted Justin up onto his shoulder, 'Back upstairs,' he said to Madison. He tried not to run as they moved through the corridors and back onto the ward in long strides.

'Sister Lee,' Fletch said sharply as they entered, 'can I have some assistance, please?'

He laid Justin on a free bed as Madison pulled the curtains around, clearly trying not to panic.

Rui Lee appeared swiftly, and demonstrated her years of experience. Unhooking the wires from the nearby cardiac monitor, clipping them onto Justin's chest and slipping a probe onto his finger. She glanced at the results and lifted the oxygen mask from the wall, turning it on in one simultaneous move. 'Fletch,' she said under her breath.

He looked at the reading as he unwound his stethoscope and spoke in a low voice. 'Justin, it's Fletch. I'm just going to listen to your chest.'

He placed his stethoscope on Justin's small chest and instantly heard something he didn't want to. He manoeuvred Justin forward and listened to his back too. 'I need an ECG, a chest X-ray and an echocardiogram.'

'What is it?' Madison's hand was on his arm.

'I'm hearing a pericardial rub. I suspect Justin has developed pericarditis. We'll do some further tests and arrange treatment.'

'Temp's fine,' said Rui after inserting an ear thermometer in Justin's ear. She arranged Justin propped up against some pillows, clearly knowing that children with pericarditis weren't comfortable being flat.

Fletch nodded and pulled up an electric prescribing tablet. 'Let's start with some steroids while we await the rest of the tests.'

Justin curled up onto his side, and Fletch gave Madison a sign. 'Do you want to get up on the bed with him?' She nodded and gratefully climbed up, hugging her son close.

Fletch could sense the frustration building inside him. What on earth was wrong with Justin?

As Madison curled around her son, her phone slipped from her pocket and landed on the floor.

Fletch bent to pick it up and froze at the picture on the screen. It was a screensaver of Justin and Mia, in long grass with—what must be their Scottish grandparents. He tilted his head to the side as something came into his head.

'Ticks,' he said.

'What?' asked Madison.

He turned the screen to her. 'Scotland. There are ticks in Scotland. What about the area that your parents stay in? Are there any around there?'

Madison frowned. 'Well, yes, I guess so. But ticks?' She was shaking her head.

Fletch pointed to the long grass. 'Ticks carry Lyme disease. It's a long shot. But maybe that's what's wrong with Justin. Could he have been bitten?'

'Yes, I suppose so. But my mum and dad would have noticed that. Don't ticks leave a big mark?'

He held up his hands, 'Some tick bites leave a red ring called erythema migrans— a rash like a bullseye, but it can also just be a rash. It can appear anything between three days and three months.'

'We didn't see anything on his skin before.'

He nodded. 'I know. But we can check again.' He took a breath. 'So, if an adult presented with joint pains, tiredness, irritation, and gave a history of travel somewhere, we might ask them if they had been bitten.'

'What if my parents don't remember?'

'Not everyone knows they've been bitten by a tick. There's a blood test we can try, but it doesn't always show positive.'

Madison bottom lip started to tremble. 'So, what does this mean for Justin? Long term?'

Fletch held up his hand. 'Let's take this slow. Let's check his body again first. Everywhere, including all the creases. Then, I'll phone and organise the ELISA test. We can also consider starting him on antibiotics.'

'Even though he doesn't have a temperature.'

Fletch nodded. 'If the first test comes back positive, we would start him on the antibiotics, while we wait for the second test.'

'How long does it take?'

'That's the hard part. It can take several days to two weeks to get the results. If we work on the assumption that Justin was bitten when he was with your parents, it could be at least seven weeks since the disease entered his system. There is a chance that he will have formed antibodies because it's been more than a few weeks. We could also test Justin's cerebrospinal fluid, but we'd need to do a lumbar puncture and I'm not sure he would tolerate that right now.'

'If we can avoid it at all, I'd rather do that.'

'What about Mia?' Fletch asked. 'I think I would like to check her over, just to be cautious and take some blood from her too. Now, she's had no symptoms, nothing that gives me concern. But let's just be sure.'

Madison gave a tearful nod. 'Okay.' She looked around and then shook her head. 'I can't go and get her from crèche right now.'

'I'll go,' Fletch said.

Madison was starting to think straighter now. 'I'll need to speak to my parents, and Jason's. I need to let them know what's happened.'

Rui Lee came back with some pyjamas for Justin and a soft blanket. She nodded to

Madison. 'Swap places with me, and go over there and make your calls.'

Madison gave a nod, and Fletch let her walk over to the window, glancing at the other faces in the room. Even though people knew about them now, they'd been very careful at not being affectionate around each other in their workplace setting. It was unprofessional, and they didn't want anyone to think their relationship might impact on their jobs.

And while Fletch knew that, and believed in all those fundamentals, at a time like this he couldn't leave Madison when she looked so distressed. He walked over and circled his arms around her, holding her tight. She sagged into him and, for a few moments, started to sob.

He held her. Just held her, until she'd finally sobbed herself out. Then he could feel her shuddering as she caught her breath. He stroked her hair for a few moments longer before catching Rui's eye.

Rui nodded to him, giving him an appreciative smile. And the smile was like a seal of approval he'd been waiting for.

He gave Madison another few moments to gather herself, and then moved to get back to Justin, speaking quietly to him as he inserted a cannula and gave him some intravenous steroids. He half wanted to climb up onto the bed himself and cuddle him, but he'd promised to collect Mia and check her over too.

His colleague Dr Zhang, another of the paediatricians, appeared and Fletch spoke rapidly to him, handing over Justin's care while he left to pick up Mia.

The crèche staff were all over him as soon as he arrived, asking how Justin was. He explained as best he could, letting them know he'd been admitted to the ward, and that he was there to pick up Mia and take her back to Madison.

Mia was clearly quite confused and upset. It was a different view of the normally confident little girl he was used to. He spoke calmly to her, and told her she could see Justin and then they were going to do some checks on her, once her mother was with her.

'Is Rui there?' asked the little voice.

He understood that. This little girl was reaching out for some familiarity. 'Yes, Rui's there. She's helping look after Justin.'

'Is Justin sleeping again?'

Fletch looked at Mia. She understood more than she probably should. 'He might be. He's very tired. But we hope we know what's wrong with him, and can make him better.'

He was already full of self-doubts. Firstly, about himself. He'd known right from the start that the twins had been in Scotland, but ticks and Lyme disease had never once entered his head until he'd seen the children's smiling faces in the long grass. He was kicking himself.

And what if this was the wrong diagnosis? Lyme disease was tricky to diagnose with the actual known presence of a tick, or the distinguishable rash. There was likely a whole host of adults in the world who had a range of symptoms caused by Lyme disease that had never been diagnosed properly.

He didn't even want to think about the amount of people bitten as a child, unnoticed, who then had a lifetime of symptoms that affected their life.

But what if it was something else?

He was sure about the pericarditis. He'd heard the rub. By the time he reached the ward, the cardiac technician had appeared and the ECG was complete and the echocardiogram under way. Madison was instantly relieved to see Mia and hugged her too, still holding onto Justin's hand as he got his echocardiogram. Rui was on his other side, talking quietly to him.

Fletch's eyes turned to the screen, and

he leaned forward and spoke softly to the technician. She pointed to a few parts on the grey screen that showed the inflamed sac surrounding the heart, along with some extra fluid. In some cases, the fluid could be drained, but, in Justin's case, they would put him on steroids and antibiotics first, to see if they made any difference. He might also need some pain relief.

Fletch was clear. This was new. When he'd examined Justin before, there had been no signs of pericarditis. It made him more confident in the potential Lyme disease diagnosis, because of the length of time from potential infection, and the subsequent inflammation that could have occurred in Justin's body.

He looked over to Madison. 'We've confirmed the diagnosis of pericarditis and we'll treat Justin for this meantime. The blood test is ordered too, and, because of the pericarditis, and the fact that Justin has complained of joint pains, I think there is a chance that the ELISA may be positive. If it is, we move to the next stage.'

Madison turned her phone around. She'd obviously been doing an Internet search. 'The list is incredible, severe fatigue, insomnia, headaches, impaired concentration, inability to sustain attention, difficulty thinking and expressing, joint pains, brain fog.' She held up her phone, her arm shaking. 'How could I not even think of this?'

He reached up and pulled down her arm. 'Madison, have you even heard of Lyme disease before?'

She shook her head in frustration. 'I don't know. I can't remember.'

'Then how are you supposed to know about it? It's easy when someone tells you, but figuring out for yourself is hard.' He took a breath. 'Did you get your parents?'

She nodded and started to cry. 'They don't remember Justin being bitten by a tick. The kids did play in the grass, just about every day, and Mum bathed them both every night. She thinks Justin had a tiny rash under his arm that disappeared when she put some cream on it. She didn't mention it because she thought it was just a sweat rash. Just nothing. She's beside herself. She wants to come over. She and Dad are looking for flights.'

Fletch swallowed. 'And what about Jason's family?'

'They're on their way. His mum got really agitated. She doesn't really understand ticks and Lyme disease. She kept asking about dogs. I couldn't really answer the questions that she had.'

Fletch touched her arm. 'I can do that. I can answer their questions.' He nodded to Rui. 'Are we able to cope on the ward if Justin has more visitors?'

Rui was usually strict about there being only two visitors at a time for children, and only the carer allowed to stay overnight. She was conscious that so many children had sensory or neurological disorders, and the hospital environment itself was overwhelming, without adding lots more people into the mix.

'Rui is going to swap Justin into another room. There are two children in this room who are going to Theatre tomorrow and she wants to keep things calm for them.'

Fletch glanced around. 'Okay, I'll give her a hand, but then we need to check Mia over. Okay?'

It took longer than he thought to get Justin moved to another room on the ward. Another patient became unwell and he had to deal with them first. By the time they'd finally got Justin settled into another room, he'd sipped some fluids and fallen asleep again, Madison looked as if she'd run a marathon.

He picked up Mia in his arms and reached over and touched Madison's cheek. 'Let's check our girl over. Then I'll go and get you some things from home so you can stay to-night.'

'But what about Mia? What will I do with her?'

'I can stay with Mia. If the ward stays like this, she can sleep in the bed next to Justin.'

A voice came from behind them. 'Madison?' It was a mixture of panic, and a very big question. Fletch dropped his hand, but not before he'd met the angry eyes of an older Singapore man.

Madison literally crumpled beneath his eyes. She became a crying, blubbering parent, trying to say too many words all at once, with none of them coming out coherently.

The man marched across the room, glared at Fletch and took Madison into his arms as a slim woman rushed into the room, to Justin's side.

Rui Lee started speaking calmly to them both in a mixture of Malaysian and English. Mia was upset. She could see both of her grandparents and her mother, and knew that they were all upset, so she started crying too. Fletch tried to shush her and rock her, but the grandmother came over and took her off him.

He was left standing in the middle of the floor as a family drama he was very much not part of, unfolded in front of him. Talk about feeling awkward.

He let himself stay calm, and moved into doctor mode. He was joined by Dr Zhang, and, between them, they explained about Justin's condition and potential diagnosis. Fletch noticed that both grandparents shot most of their questions to his colleague—almost as if he weren't there. Madison seemed numb. It was as if, now that other people were here to take over, she'd finally shut down in the way her body and mind had probably wanted to do when she'd realised what was wrong with her son.

He got that. She spent so much of her life holding things together. No one could do that indefinitely. Not even the amazing resilient woman that he was growing to love.

The reality hit him like a slap in the face. He loved her. He'd known from the first moment he met Madison that there was something different about her, and the connection he felt, and now he recognised it for what it was.

He loved this woman. He wished he could wave a magic wand and make things better for her. For her, and for Justin.

The thoughts overwhelmed him. And it wasn't the time, or the place. Fletch knew that.

He could have time to have this conversation with Madison at any point in the future. No matter how he felt at this moment, he had to be the best doctor possible for Justin. That was how he could do the most for Maddie now.

He swallowed, trying to gather his thoughts and keep them away from the situation.

But he couldn't. And he knew the first impression he'd made with Jason's family wouldn't help. These people were so important to Madison and her children, and he had to try and keep things as stable as possible for her.

Fletch kept everything professional and let them know that he still had to take some time to examine Mia. Madison was on the bed holding Justin, so he asked Mrs Koh if she would accompany Mia while he examined her.

Mrs Koh looked reluctant to begin with, but when Dr Zhang agreed and encouraged her that it could happen in the room next door, and wouldn't take long, she finally relented.

Fletch was his normal self with Mia. He chatted as he examined her, checking her skin, looking for any sign of a rash, and listening to her heart and lungs. He asked her to do some jumps and bends, asking if anything was sore or hurting. He knew she'd been eating and drinking well—he'd seen that for himself. And there was nothing in her demeanour that gave him any cause for concern.

As he went along, he explained to Mrs Koh about the symptoms Justin had been having and how they could possibly relate to the diagnosis of Lyme disease. He reassured her that Mia showed no signs of anything similar, and, although she remained guarded with him the whole time, she was polite.

When Mia was dressed again, she climbed up onto Fletch's lap instead of her grandmother's and leaned into him. 'Is Justin going to be okay?'

Fletch's brain did that split-second thing of weighing up all possibilities. If he seemed overfamiliar with this child, Jason's mother would know there was more to his and Madison's relationship. If he set her down on the floor, without comforting her, he could upset Mia. There wasn't really a choice.

He stroked her hair and spoke in a low voice to her. 'Justin needs to stay in hospital tonight. And so does Mummy. But if he stays tonight, and maybe tomorrow, he'll start to feel better soon. I hope we can find a way to stop him feeling so tired all the time.'

'Then he'll play more?' she asked brightly.

A child's perspective and very Mia, straight to the point.

'I hope he will,' answered Fletch, 'but it might take a little time for him to feel better again.'

He could almost feel Mrs Koh's cool gaze on him, but he wasn't letting himself be awkward around Mia. It wasn't fair on her, and she wouldn't understand.

Mia turned back to and put her arms out towards Mrs Koh, murmuring, 'Nenek,' and Fletch handed her back over. He gave a nod to Mrs Koh. 'Let's tell Madison that there's nothing to worry about regarding Mia.'

The woman gave him the briefest nod and carried Mia on her hip as they walked back through.

Madison was still upset, and Justin looked plain exhausted. Fletch caught Rui's gaze and as he opened his mouth to stay something that would make him even more unpopular, Rui got there before him.

'Mrs Koh, do you want a few moments with Justin? I really need some peaceful time for him, so he can sleep, and hopefully the medicines will start to take effect. Could you and Mr Koh then take Mia down to the staff canteen and get her something to drink?'

Rui had a manner that meant no one would ever argue. Fletch saw something flash in Mr Koh's eyes as if he was contemplating it for a second. But he looked around the rest of his room, his scowl saved solely for Fletch, and gave a nod of his head. He touched Madison's arm, but Rui spoke again. 'Please take Madison with you too. She needs a few minutes away from the ward, and a chance to talk to Mia.'

Mr Koh was slightly surprised by these added words, but bent to kiss his grandson, then wrapped his arm around Madison in a fatherly way and led her out of the room.

Fletch felt useless.

Madison looked broken. He wanted to be with her. Help her. Stay alongside her every step of the way.

But Rui stepped in front of him.

'She's in shock. She needs time out. She's held things together for so long since Jason died, and this—this is the thing that's tipped her.'

Fletch took a long slow breath. 'I want to help her.'

'I know you do. But the best way to help Madison right now is to look after her son.'

He looked back at little Justin and his heart ached. 'I've let Justin down too. I should have thought of Lyme disease earlier.'

'Why? We don't have it in Singapore. It's extremely rare. Why would you consider it?'

He was angry with himself. 'Because the children were in Scotland. I *knew* that. And I didn't make the connection.'

'But Lyme disease is still quite rare there too. You can't second-guess yourself here, Fletch. Another paediatrician might not have made the connection that you did.'

He sat down next to Justin and stroked his hand. 'I hate seeing him like this.'

Rui gave him a knowing smile. 'That's because you've formed an attachment.'

He opened his mouth to deny it automatically, then realised there was no point. 'Yes, I have.' He sighed and looked at her. 'Madison was going to tell Jason's parents about us, but it's clear she's not done that. Maybe she's changed her mind about us.'

As he said the words out loud, he finally understood the kind of impact this had on him. He'd spent the last few weeks fretting about taking the next step. Worrying if he was ready. Wondering what would happen if things didn't work out, instead of just committing to the family that he'd found and clearly loved.

Was it any wonder that Madison had doubts too? He wondered what life had been really like for her for the last three years. Being widowed and left with two babies, only months old. Twins were notoriously hard on any parents, but on a single parent, who was also grieving? And while she'd had a support system when she'd asked for help—he somehow knew that he could likely count on one hand the amount of times Madison had actually done so.

Even now, when she wasn't getting a full night's sleep due to Justin's insomnia, she still turned up to work every day with a smile on her face, and commitment to her patients and her colleagues.

And, in amongst all that, she'd tried to make some time for him. Some time for herself, to try and get a little of her life back. He had nothing but admiration for this woman.

He gave a sad smile to Rui. 'Some people would tell me I was punching above my weight.'

'Some people would be right,' she added without hesitation, then put her hand on his shoulder. 'But you're not so bad, Fletch. I'm just waiting to see how you shape up.'

'I'm not entirely sure I'm going to get the chance. I don't think Jason's family like me.'

'They don't know you. And Madison should have warned them she was seeing someone else. They just dashed here after finding out their grandson was very sick. That's the thing that's front and centre in their mind right now—not you,' she said simply, clearly putting him back in his box for a while.

Fletch could not remember a time that he'd wanted people to like him so much. It was so outside his normal range of thought. He really needed to get some perspective.

He needed a chance to make sure that Madison was okay. But didn't want to make things worse for her. Rui seemed to read his mind. 'Patience,' she said simply. 'I'm going to get Dr Zhang to review some of our other patients while you stay with Justin.' She glanced down at the fragile sleeping child. 'I think he'll be happy that you're there with him,' she said as she walked out of the room.

Fletch looked down at the little chest rising and falling and the ticking on the monitor. If he had only one wish right now, it was to have found the correct diagnosis for Justin, and for him to get better.

The wish wouldn't be for him, nor for Madison. It would be for this tiny little boy next to him, who deserved a lifetime of good health.

CHAPTER TEN

SHE'D BLINKED AND her life had folded in on itself. That was the only thing she could think.

So much had happened so quickly that there simply wasn't time to process any of it.

First and forefront in her mind was Justin. Her son was sick.

Yes, she'd known for a few weeks that something was wrong, but she'd never expected this. The call from the crèche had been a bolt from the blue. And seeing Fletch carrying her limp child had just about been the end of her.

After that, things had just kind of disappeared into a cloud.

This wasn't her. This wasn't her at all. Madison had always been calm in a crisis. She'd prided herself on that fact. But now? She didn't even know what time it was. She was conscious of Mia in her lap, her arms around her, and the fact she was rocking back and forward.

Even when she'd got the news about Jason's accident, life hadn't been like this.

She'd had a few moments of disbelief. Of horror. And complete shock. But then her survival skills had kicked in.

She'd had babies to care for, a funeral to organise and mourning to do. People had been around her. Food had appeared at her door. Family members had been there to hold her hand on the day of the funeral. The amount of paperwork had taken more than a year to sort out. Wills, bank accounts, insurance, medical records—some of the apparently simple things, like switching names on utility bills, had been the most frustrating of all.

Letters still occasionally arrived with Jason's name on them. Usually from nondescript companies where his name and address had been sold to some mailing list. But she'd got there. She'd managed all that. Jason had been a fellow adult. And while he'd been her husband and she'd loved him, her brain had managed to accept that sometimes accidents happened—even though it seemed immensely unfair.

She hadn't been out on a mission of vengeance. The Singapore authorities had investigated the incident and charged someone with reckless driving. It had been a first-time offence. The person had been temporarily blinded by the sun for a few seconds. It was honestly and truly an accident, and Madison and Jason's family had all accepted that.

But this? This couldn't even compute. This was their child. A part of them. Of course, the kids had been sick before. But not like this. Not with something that could be serious. Lyme disease could have lasting effects on those affected. Pericarditis could have unexpected implications.

It could be irregular heartbeats, or require more serious interventions like surgery. And with surgery, there were always further risks.

Because Madison worked in a hospital, her brain automatically went to the worst-case scenario. She could lose her child. Unthinkable. The words that Fletch had said to her at one point stuck in her head. *'No parent should outlive their child.'* And all of a sudden she was ready to be sick.

She pushed Mia towards her grandparents and dashed to the hospital toilets. Her whole body was shaking, and after she retched, she splashed her face with cold water, and leaned against the tiled wall, thankful for the coolness seeping through her scrubs.

She had to get back to Justin. She had to be by his side. Why was she even down here? Panic gripped her again and as she rushed back out of the door Jason's father was waiting for her. He was calm. Just as she should be.

He put a hand on either side of her shoulder. 'Stop, Madison, just breathe.'

She blinked as tears rolled down her face. 'I have to get back to Justin.'

'You will, just not like this.'

She knew he made sense, but she still didn't like the words. They were keeping her from her son.

'Justin is being looked after.'

His lips tightened at the words, and she knew exactly what he was thinking. *By that man*. The man who had been touching her cheek when Mr and Mrs Koh had come into the room, and clearly been shocked.

The man she'd promised that she would start the conversation with Jason's parents around dating again.

Something she hadn't done. Because she hadn't been brave enough.

She'd seen the reaction. Fletch clearly knew that she'd given them no warning because it had been blatantly obvious. Jason's parents were unfailingly polite and she'd put them in a terrible position. It was bad enough that their grandson was sick, without simultaneously throwing a potential new relationship into the mix. It was disrespectful, and she'd never, ever wanted to do that to them.

'I… I'm sorry,' she started. 'I should explain. The doctor…'

Mr Koh held up his hand. It was as if a mask had appeared over his face. 'You don't need to tell us. And it's not the time.'

He was right. On both counts. But she wanted to tell him, she didn't want to keep things from her in-laws.

'Everything is new,' she said quietly, as she felt tears come to her eyes again. 'I just wasn't sure I was ready.'

'And are you?' It was the tone of the words. She knew this man. She'd known him for more than ten years. This wasn't him. But he'd never been in this position before, and neither had she. Neither of them was handling this well. The answer to the question was stuck on her lips.

Her heart squeezed inside her chest. She didn't want to hurt her in-laws. She loved them and she needed them. And her brain was so confused right now. She needed to focus on her son, and only her son, until they could get through all this.

'N…no,' she breathed.

There was a noise to her right. It was Fletch. He'd come looking for her. Probably because she'd been so upset when she left the ward.

But his face was made of stone. He'd heard. He blinked, and he turned on his heel and walked away.

Fletch was numb.

He wouldn't think about this. He wouldn't. But he'd heard her truth. She'd said she wasn't ready.

And against all hope his heart was truly broken.

It wasn't as if she hadn't warned him at the beginning. And it was kind of ridiculous that he'd needed to witness this to finally get the message. He should have grasped it a few hours earlier when he'd realised that she hadn't told her in-laws she was dating again. The two things went hand in hand.

Now, he had to put his feelings aside and do his job. Likely under the scrutiny of all his colleagues, who would know exactly what was happening.

But that was the thing. He didn't actually care about his colleagues' thoughts. He didn't want to concentrate on that at all.

He wanted to walk back in and plead with Madison to rethink. To think about spending the rest of her life with Fletch and their children.

His skin prickled and he swallowed, his throat achingly dry. This was so not the time for thoughts like these. He had a child to take care of. Test results to wait for, and likely further tests to do. Whatever else happened, and no matter how much Mr and Mrs Koh disapproved of him, he had a duty of care to that little boy to give him the best outcome possible.

He'd always known at some point he'd get his heart broken. Maybe he deserved this? Maybe his own break-ups in the past hadn't been as amicable as he'd thought. Just because he'd been honest, didn't mean that his exes hadn't been hurt. Had he been naïve all along?

Was this why he always held back? Was this why he never wanted to commit— because he couldn't deal with a broken heart? But no one had felt like Madison to him. No one had given him such strong vibes and good connections. No one had made his heart sing as she did. No one else's smile could light the day as hers could.

Was it worth it? Was it worth feeling that connection only to have it ripped away again? Because right now he just wasn't sure.

He breathed slowly. This was a hospital. His personal feelings had to be set aside here, in order for him to do the job he was supposed to do. But it was hard. Harder than he could ever have imagined.

He tilted his chin and clenched his fists, urging his body to let him hide these emotions and play the ultimate professional, just as he should.

As he made his way back to the ward his mind was set. He was a doctor. That was what he was. And all he would concentrate on the for the near future.

CHAPTER ELEVEN

LIFE HAD COLLAPSED around her like a house of cards.

One minute she'd been on the brink of starting something new and exciting, the next, her kid was sick, her life upside down, and her relationship with her in-laws at risk because she hadn't treated them with the respect they deserved.

Could she have got things any more wrong?

Well, yes. The look in Fletch's eyes when he'd heard her say she wasn't ready had been enough to pierce her heart.

She hadn't meant it. She really hadn't. But she just couldn't say something different to Jason's dad.

And she should have. She should have been honest. But did the fact she couldn't be honest mean her brain was telling her she wasn't ready?

Madison had never been so confused in her life.

She was living her life in a bubble right now. Her parents had arrived, guilt-stricken and worried sick over Justin.

His ELISA test had come back positive, and now they were doing a Western blot test. If it was also positive, then, along with Justin's other symptoms, he would be diagnosed with Lyme disease.

His condition had started to pick up. The steroids had helped his pericarditis and he'd also been started on antibiotics. Her little boy was still tired, but starting to seem more like himself again.

Mia had been a whirlwind of activity, going between two sets of grandparents who were all delighted to spend time with her. She was living her best life.

As for Fletch? He barely met Madison's gaze.

He was still doing his job. He was attentive and kind to Justin. He'd spent more than an hour with her parents from Scotland, explaining the disease and reassuring them that lots of people got bitten by ticks, developed Lyme disease and didn't remember the bite. It waylaid their fears that they'd been neglectful with their grandchildren and Justin's illness was their fault.

She could still see her mum's hands kneading together on her lap, and knew that no words would probably really placate them, but Fletch had tried his best and she was grateful for that.

At times, she tried to catch him, to try and get a few moments to apologise for what he'd witnessed. But he'd clearly made his mind up that the conversation between them was not going to happen.

Rui kept giving her careful glances, obviously realising how anxious she was, but not able to have that conversation with her either, because of all the people around.

Finally, as Justin perked up day by day, Dr Zhang and Fletch decided he could be discharged. She wept with relief. It had been the longest ten days of her life.

His pericarditis was gone—for now—and he would continue to be monitored for any other symptoms connected to Lyme disease meantime. It was hoped that the antibiotics would fight off the effects and lessen the chance of any further symptoms.

When she finally walked through the doors of her apartment again, she gave a huge sigh of relief. Her mum and dad were staying, and luggage was everywhere.

She was just so glad to be home again.

As she tried to find some kind of routine, feeding and bathing the children, then getting them to bed, her eyes kept drifting to the sofa. The sofa where she'd sat on a few occasions with Fletch. It seemed empty without him, and she wondered how the space in the apartment would feel once her parents were gone again.

'What's wrong?' her mother asked when she finally sat down.

'Oh, nothing, and everything.' She sighed.

'What do you mean?'

Madison ran her hands through her hair. When was the last time she'd washed it?

She stared out over the view she loved. Although her parents had invited her to come back and stay in Scotland on numerous occasions, she'd never felt the pull. Her home was Singapore, she wanted to stay here, and was worried that anything she might say might just make them pressure her to move home again.

'What would you say if I told you that I'd met someone else?'

Her mother's mouth fell open for a second. 'Oh, well... I guess I'd ask who it is.'

'You've met him,' said Madison, before she lost her courage.

'It's been three years,' said her father's reasonable voice. 'We've never expected you to spend the rest of your life alone.'

'But is it too soon?' She turned to face him.

'Only you can answer that,' he replied, ever the diplomat.

'What about Mia and Justin?' asked her mother. 'Have they met this person?'

Madison nodded. 'Yes, and they like him. And he likes them. Everything seemed…to be going well…' Her voice drifted off.

'So, what changed?' asked her father.

'All this,' she said in exasperation.

'Well, if they can't stay around for the hard stuff, are they really the right person for you?' asked her mother. It was a reasonable observation, but Madison couldn't let it lie.

'I pushed him away,' she said as the full realisation swept over her. 'Things were just so complicated with Jason's parents there, and they didn't know I was dating anyone, and they saw him touch me, and I got upset—because I didn't want to upset them, and…' Her shoulders started to shake.

'It's Justin's doctor, isn't it?' asked her dad. Madison's head shot up.

He gave her a half-smile. 'I noticed things. The way the children related to him, the way he looked at you.'

She sagged her head into her hands. 'I meant to tell Jason's parents I was thinking about dating again. No, I meant to tell them I *was* dating again. But I just couldn't find the words. I can see Jason in both of their faces. I didn't want them to think I had forgotten. That I had moved on without considering how they would feel.'

She shook her head. 'I've made a whole mess of this. I got in a jumble. Mr Koh saw Fletch touching me. I think he was angry. And with Justin so sick… I just told him I wasn't ready and Fletch heard that.'

'It's a misunderstanding,' said her dad. 'You were under a lot of stress.'

She lifted her gaze. 'But I hurt him.'

Her mother looked at her. 'You did. But you know it. And you need to be big enough to have that conversation. How do you feel about him?'

The question from her mother hit home. And she was almost glad her mother had put her on the spot, to make her say the words out loud.

'I love him.' The words were sure. Because that was exactly how she felt.

She took a deep breath. 'But I haven't told him that. Not yet.' She blinked back tears. 'But I hope that he knows. We did talk. We talked about being together.' Her lip trembled. 'Since Jason died, I never thought I would feel like this about anyone else. I never thought I would really find love again.' The more she spoke, the more she realised exactly how much this all meant to her. Exactly how much was at stake. 'I don't want to mess this up.' Her voice broke and her mother reached over and put her arm around her daughter's shoulders.

'Then don't.' Her mother smiled. She gave her a squeeze. 'We want you to be happy, you and the kids. Find your happiness, Madison, and hold on tight.'

CHAPTER TWELVE

HE LOVED SINGAPORE. He wanted to stay here. But he couldn't imagine seeing Madison on a daily basis and not being with her. The thought made every bone in his body ache. So, he started looking at other jobs, other places to be.

He was considering one in Missouri when Rui came into the office. Astute as ever, she saw the job advert straight away.

'You're not leaving. I thought your contract was for two years.'

'It is.' He sighed. 'But I'm not sure I can stay any longer.'

'I'm not sure you deserve to,' she quipped back.

He turned around his chair incredulously. 'What?'

She folded her arms.

He shook his head. 'Madison told her in-laws that she wasn't ready to move on. The message was clear. I just don't think I can spend the rest of my time here without having mixed emotions. This is her permanent job, her permanent home. I don't want things to be awkward for her. She loves her work, and I don't want to get in the way.'

'So, the easiest solution is to walk away?'

'It seems like the kindest thing to do.'

Rui snorted. 'Kind? If you walk away you'll break her heart!'

'How can you possibly say that?'

She walked over to him. 'Tell me this. Do you really think she could answer that question honestly, when she was under so much pressure? You saw her up here. She'd unravelled, completely. Okay, so she hadn't told her in-laws yet about you. And yes, she should have. But she's walking a fine line, of balancing her relationship with them and creating a new one with you. If she'd told them downstairs in the canteen that, yes, she was ready to move on, and with the new doctor who was treating their grandchild, don't you think that would have been a blow like a hammerhead?'

He sat back. 'Maybe, well…yes. But what if it also gave her the opportunity to be truthful to herself that she wasn't ready? Maybe I pushed her when I shouldn't have. This might have been a soft way out for her.'

'You really believe that?' The scepticism in her voice was heavy. Rui folded her arms. 'Let me tell you something. Madison is a coper. That's what she's done ever since Jason died. She's coped. These last few weeks were the first time I saw some sparkle in her eyes again, some real life about her. I caught the way she was looking at you— long before either of you admitted something was going on. I've watched you with those children. They adore you. And you're great with them. Sure, it's only been a few months, but there is time here, Fletch. There's a real chance for you both, and you'd be a fool to throw that away.'

His insides twisted. He so wanted all of this to be true.

He shook his head. 'I know what I want, but I don't know if it's what Madison wants. And what about Jason's parents? It is quite clear they don't like me. She has a good relationship with them. I don't want to ruin that for her.'

Rui gave a slow nod. 'It's not about picking a side. It's about being honest. They walked into a scene they didn't bank on seeing, at a time of crisis in their family life.' Her mouth pressed together. 'These are good people, Fletch. They will never get their son back, and, long term, they will want the absolute best for Madison and the kids. You just need to persuade them that the best—is you.'

He straightened in his chair and gave her a smile. It was the first time he'd felt hopeful in the last ten days. 'You realise this could all go horribly wrong, and I could make a fool of myself?'

She shrugged her shoulders in an amused way and nodded.

He grinned. 'But she's worth it. *They're* worth it.'

'Of course, they are,' she agreed.

And without another second of hesitation, Fletch picked up his jacket and walked out.

He kept telling himself he was doing the right thing, even though his stomach seemed to clench and release at regular intervals. By the time he'd crossed the city and reached the quieter street it seemed as though he was the only person around. He checked the address again and walked up to the door before he could change his mind.

He rang the bell and waited, hearing footsteps inside before Mrs Koh opened the door. Her eyes widened slightly in surprise. He gave a small bow. 'Mrs Koh, I wonder if I could have a moment of your time, please?'

She paused for a second before opening the door and gesturing him inside, calling to her husband. As she invited him to sit on a cream chair, her husband came through. The surprise was evident on his face. 'What is this?' he asked, before quickly asking, 'Justin?'

Fletch raised his hand. 'Justin is fine. He is at home with his mother, and his other grandparents.'

The Kohs looked at each other and gave a nod before sitting opposite Fletch, with their hands folded in their laps.

It was like being called to the headmaster's office, and Fletch had to remind himself he'd chosen to do this.

'Thank you for speaking to me. I wanted to talk to you both and Madison, and Mia and Justin. First of all, I wanted to apologise for how you found us in the hospital. I've become very close to Madison and the children since I came to Singapore, and was trying to comfort Madison when you arrived.'

Mrs Koh shifted a little uncomfortably, and Mr Koh's face remained fixed.

He continued, 'I want you to know that I love Madison. I love Justin and Mia too.

They are wonderful, and I feel very lucky to have found them.' He paused, taking a deep breath, wondering if this was where everything would go wrong.

'So, I wanted to ask your approval to be involved in their lives. Madison loves you both so much. And I realise that you will be protective over your daughter-in-law, and your grandchildren. I want to promise you that I will love and protect them to the best of my ability.' He swallowed and licked his lips, before breaking into a smile. 'They are very, very special.'

'They are,' agreed Mrs Koh, her gaze cautious.

There was a very long silence. 'Why did you come here?' asked Mr Koh.

Fletch relaxed his tense shoulders. 'Because I wanted to be honest with you. I love Madison. I won't let her go without a fight. I'm sorry if the thought of her moving on is hurtful to you both. I can only promise you that I'm sincere. And if I'm to become part of Madison and the children's lives, I hope I can become part of yours too.'

He held his breath. Wondering if he'd just taken a step too far.

After the longest time, Mr Koh stood up. He took a few steps towards Fletch and held out his hand. Fletch breathed the biggest sigh of relief and stood up to shake it.

'Thank you for coming to see us,' said Mr Koh.

Mrs Koh gave a small nod of her head.

'Thank you,' said Fletch, not trying to hide his smile. 'Now I guess I have to go and speak to Madison.'

'You came here first?' asked Mr Koh, his eyebrows raised.

'I did.'

Mr Koh tilted his head slightly in question. 'And if I'd told you no?'

Fletch gave him a smile. 'I would have respectfully told you that Madison and the kids were worth fighting for, and that I would still try.'

Mr Koh gave an amused smile. 'Well, I'm glad we've come to an understanding.'

'So am I.'

This time as he walked down the street it seemed brighter and full of life. Now, all he had to do was convince the woman that he loved that they were worth fighting for.

And he knew exactly how to do it.

CHAPTER THIRTEEN

Madison looked at the text on her phone again.

Meet me at the bandstand at eleven a.m. Fletch x.

Her eyes kept going back to the kiss. That had to be good, right? And the fact he was asking to meet her must mean he was ready to talk.

She'd been nervous when she received the text this morning, and had spent more than an hour deciding what to wear. Finally, she settled on a pink shirt and white skirt and a pair of flat shoes.

It wasn't high heels. But she wasn't sure if it was a high heels kind of day. She knew exactly what she wanted to say. She wanted to tell him that she loved him. She wanted to tell him how sorry she was that she'd said those words in the hospital, and could only hope that he might forgive her. She wanted to start her life over, and she wanted to do that with Fletch.

She was sure there would still be mistakes, still be misunderstandings. But she could live with that. They could work through them. Only she hoped they could.

What if this was something else entirely? What if he wanted to say they would be best being friends and just leave it at that? He'd done that in previous relationships in the past, and it might be her actions had made him think that she didn't really care about him.

Her nerves were jittery as she approached the bandstand in the Botanical Gardens. At first, she thought he wasn't there. But as she drew closer, she saw that he was. He just wasn't standing at the railing, he was sitting down inside.

Her heart felt as if it hiccupped. She put her hand on the railing. 'Fletch?' she said in a quiet voice.

His dark head lifted. His gaze was cautious. 'Hey.'

She moved inside the bandstand, looked around, then sat down next to him. 'What are we doing in here?'

'I wanted to come somewhere we had good memories.'

She gulped, worried about how this might go. 'I want to say sorry. For what I said in the hospital. I was put on the spot and I just didn't know what to do. I hadn't got around to having the conversation I wanted to, then, in the middle of all that, I felt as if I couldn't say it out loud.'

Fletch gave a nod of his head. 'I wonder if that means more than you think it does.'

She shook her head, but Fletch put his hand on her arm.

'Madison, I know how I feel. I know how I feel about you and the kids. But, if things start, I want them to start the right way. And I wonder if your brain, or your heart, was telling you something that you hadn't quite faced yourself.'

She was stunned at his words, and tried to digest them. Could they possibly be true?

She took a deep breath and put her hand on her chest. 'My heart and brain are quite sure how they feel. I was just a distressed mum under pressure, that didn't handle things well. That's all it was.'

She could feel him take a shaky breath next to her. 'I need you to be sure, Maddie. Because I'm sure. I'm sure that I love you and the kids and I want to be part of your lives. I'm so sure, I went to see Mr and Mrs Koh today.'

Her mouth fell open and she turned to face him. 'What?'

He nodded. 'We met under the wrong circumstances, and I'm partly to blame for that. I wanted them to know that I'm serious about you and the kids. I wanted them to know that I love their daughter-in-law. I'm not some fly-by-night kind of guy. I also told them that I'd like to get to know them better too.'

Tears started to stream down her face. He'd done that. He'd done that for her, for Mia and for Justin. 'What did they say?'

'Mr Koh was quiet to begin with, but when I told him I wanted their approval he seemed to realise I was serious.'

She gave a surprised laugh. 'Isn't it my dad's approval you're meant to ask?'

Fletch looked her right in the eye. 'This is a different, and unique, set of circumstances. I thought this might be the best way to start with them.'

She wiped her tears away. 'And did they give it?'

He smiled. 'He asked me what I'd do if he said no.'

Her eyes widened. 'He never.'

'Oh, he did. I get the impression Mr Koh might be a bit of an old rogue. But anyway, I told him if he said no, you were still worth fighting for, and—he agreed.'

He intertwined his fingers with hers. 'So, what do you say?'

She reached up with her other hand and touched his cheek. 'I say thank you. Thank you for being understanding. Thank you for going out on a limb for us. And thank you for making the extra effort with Jason's family.'

His gaze was steady on hers. 'But that's not the part I really want to know.'

She smiled and leaned towards him. 'I love you, Arthur Fletcher. And even though you've told me you've never wanted to do this before, I'm prepared to take a chance on you.' Her voice had a joking tone.

'You are?' His other hand slid into her hair as he pulled her face towards his. He kept his voice low. 'Then you might be interested in the present I bought you.'

She pulled back. 'You bought me a present?'

He nodded his head to the other side of the bandstand where a white shoe box had blended into the surroundings. Her brow wrinkled with curiosity and she moved to pick it up, before sitting back down next to him.

'You bought me shoes?' she queried as she lifted the lid, wondering what on earth he had done.

It only took a few seconds for the realisation to hit. She lifted out a white designer high heel. But it was no ordinary high heel. It was special. It was embellished with tiny white pearls and diamantés. She let out a gasp.

'Think you could find a reason to wear these in the next year some time?'

She couldn't stop grinning as she put the shoe back in the box, and shifted onto his lap, wrapping her arms around his neck. 'Oh, I think I might be able to find a reason,' she teased. 'But you'll need to kiss me first before I decide.'

And so, he did.

EPILOGUE

'I'M FIRST,' SAID JUSTIN, elbowing Mia.

'No, I'm first,' she shot back, pushing him right back.

'Why don't you both go together?' whispered Fletch, as he set them down the path towards the bandstand, lined with friends and family.

They were almost five now, and he couldn't love them more if he tried. They both took a few steps, looked at each, then practically sprinted towards the bandstand in their race to be first.

Friends and family were all laughing, Jason's family members the most.

Fletch's father gave him a nudge. 'I like how they keep you on your toes.' He smiled.

Fletch grasped his father's hand. 'You have no idea.' He beamed.

Asking his father to be his best man and having him by his side had been a no-brainer for Fletch. His father's recovery had continued to progress well, he'd had no further strokes and he'd visited Fletch and Madison frequently in the last few years.

They walked down the path together, nodding at friends, shaking a few hands and climbing the steps to the bandstand.

Rui Lee walked down after them as Madison's matron of honour, dressed in an elegant dark blue gown.

Then the music changed, and Madison appeared in the flowered archway with her father at her side. She was wearing a traditional bridal dress, but it was simple. Pale cream satin, with some beading at the bodice, and a bouquet filled with heather and tartan ribbons. Her hair was loose and she wore no veil, but had some flowers pinned in her hair.

Fletch's breath hitched in his throat. This was it. This was the moment he'd been waiting his whole life for, and it was everything he'd hoped for.

His bride was the most beautiful woman on the planet and she couldn't hide the smile on her face as she walked towards him.

The road had been smoother than they'd thought it would be. Jason's family had been gracious and taken their time to get to know Fletch and welcome him as part of the family. Fletch's position had been made permanent, and he and Madison had bought a new house in the outskirts of the heart of Singapore.

'Hey, you,' she said as she climbed the steps of the bandstand towards him.

'Hey, you,' he replied, taking her hand and holding it close to his chest. 'Has anyone told you that you're the most beautiful bride in the world?' he said.

'I have!' shouted Mia from beneath them.

They both laughed and Madison leaned closer. 'I take it all back,' she whispered.

'About what?'

'Inviting exes to weddings. Monique, Viv and Indira are the nicest women I've ever met.'

He looked out over their friends. Monique was heavily pregnant, and with her husband. Viv had her baby on her hip, and Indira was getting married in a few months. All had been delighted to come to the wedding of the friend they'd dubbed the eternal bachelor.

The messages he'd received back had ranged from *Finally!* to, *Can't wait to meet her!* and *Let's give this lady an award!*

'I'm assuming you'll all gang up against me?' he joked.

'Already done.' Madison smiled, reaching

her hand up and touching his cheek. 'Are you ready for this?'

'Been waiting all my life,' Fletch replied without a second of hesitation.

The celebrant gave them both a nod. 'Can we get started?'

Fletch held up his hand. 'Give me one second.' He bent down and picked up Mia in one arm and Justin in the other, resting them both on his hips.

He kissed Madison's cheek. 'We're a team,' he said, 'and now we're ready.'

She looked up into the eyes of the man she loved and kissed him back. 'Yes, we are.'

* * * * *

If you enjoyed this story, check out these other great reads from Scarlet Wilson

Nurse with a Billion Dollar Secret
Snowed In with the Surgeon
The Night They Never Forgot
Neonatal Doc on Her Doorstep

All available now!